DARK UNIVERSE

DANIEL F. GALOUYE

N O T A B L E S

ARC MANOR
ROCKVILLE, MARYLAND

✳

SHAHID MAHMUD
PUBLISHER

www.CaezikSF.com

ISBN: 978-1-64710-052-0

First CAEZIK Notables Edition. First Printing. October 2022.
1 2 3 4 5 6 7 8 9 10

An imprint of Arc Manor LLC

www.CaezikSF.com

CONTENTS

INTRODUCTION: DARKNESS VISIBLE

by Richard Chwedyk

THIS NOVEL IS A MEDITATION on darkness.

It takes place in a subterranean world.

Humans have had a fascination for both as long as they have been anything recognizably human. Maybe even before.

Jules Verne, with his *Journey to the Center of the Earth*, not only gave a boost to the burgeoning field of "scientific romance," but he popularized interest in the earth sciences and the exploration of that world below our feet. Along with the networks of caves and caverns one can potentially explore, he suggested that deep below the surface one might find our world is hollow, illuminated by a molten core that acts much like the sun in our world and by microscopic bioluminescent life clinging to the rocks of its deepest chambers.

Hollow Earth theories predated Verne, but he did much to popularize them. Enough so to inspire Edgar Rice Burroughs to envision the world of Pellucidar in *At the Earth's Core* and subsequent adventure novels in the series, even sending his most famous character, Tarzan of the Apes, down there to contend with primitive humans and prehistoric creatures.

And after World War II, Raymond A. Palmer, editor of *Amazing Stories* magazine, retrieved a letter thrown into the trash by his assistant, Howard Browne. The letter was from a man, Richard Sharpe Shaver, who claimed to have evidence of an ancient Lemurian civilization still active in a labyrinthine subterranean world.

1

Palmer polished up Shaver's demented prose, adding a few lurid touches of his own, and generated a series of works, the "Shaver Mystery" which, though Palmer never claimed they were true, he emphatically stated they were not fiction. For a brief period, circulation for *Amazing Stories* shot up dramatically. Large numbers of readers wanted to believe in a world beneath the world.

And that belief could be seen in the popularity of the 1964 book, *The Hollow Earth* by "Dr. Raymond W. Bernard." Hollow Earth proponents persist in significant numbers to this day.

Lest we forget, Lewis Carroll first sent his Alice down a rabbit hole to a different sort of subterranean world of wonders.

And darkness?

We may not think so much of our prehistoric ancestors as being the cave dwellers we once believed they were, but they spent a requisite amount of time in caves, and from what they left behind we can tell that much of that time was spent in darkness.

And from the fragments of Sumerian poems we've retrieved, we have at least one account of Gilgamesh heading down into the netherworld in search of his lost friend, Enkidu.

Orpheus journeyed to the underworld to reclaim his Eurydice.

Aeneas, in Virgil's account, ventured to the underworld to find Dido.

And when Dante Alighieri, halfway through his life, takes the wrong path and ends up in a dark wood, who should he run into but Virgil? Who leads him on a path nearly to the threshold of Paradise—but begins below, in the Inferno.

We're leaving out a few dozen other important journeys, but you get the point. Many important cosmologies may look upward to the heavens, but they do not neglect that their spiritual edifices include a basement.

When Milton, in *Paradise Lost*, has God cast Satan into Hell, the fallen angel perceives:

A dungeon horrible, on all sides round,
As one great furnace flamed; yet from those flames
No light; but rather darkness visible . . .

It is that "darkness visible" that Jared Fenton, the hero of *Dark Universe*, Survivor and soon to become Prime Survivor, seems to be searching for. Milton doesn't explain the image, but seems to suggest that there may be more to darkness than the absence of light.

Horror writers have made much of this image. One example that comes to mind is from the radio play by Arch ("Lights Out") Oboler, "The Dark." A doctor and an ambulance driver arrive at an old out-of-the-way house. Within, they discover an old woman apparently out of her mind and a man "turned inside out." The madwoman indicates that the source of the horror is behind a door that the doctor, heedless of the ambulance driver's apprehension, immediately opens. "All my life, things have been what they've been. I'm gonna know all about this!" The room has no floor and is dark, but "a deeper dark than dark" spills over the edges of the hole. The dark rises "like black smoke" and makes a hissing noise before it envelopes the madwoman and turns her inside out as well. Of course, the dark gets the ambulance driver next, and finally the doctor, who observes that it crawls like shadows, like "long black fingers . . . cold, slimy—how can shadows be slimy?"

So much for horror. How can such a conception of darkness be used in a science fiction novel and, more significantly, why?

All the aforementioned subterranean worlds, excepting Milton's, seemed to have found some means of illumination to keep their denizens from walking into walls or falling into precipices.

There is an obvious irony in Jared seeking darkness while being surrounded by it, in a lightless world, where the humans of one tier can get around mostly with the aid of their highly developed hearing. Other humans, the Zivvers, have a sort of infrared vision that helps them maneuver, much like the other creatures that occupy the deepest reaches of our world.

The cause of all this, of course, is nuclear war. Survivors may believe in Light Almighty, but they also name their Satan as Radiation, aided by the twin devils Cobalt and Strontium.

The novel was published in 1961, a year before the Cuban Missile Crisis. Public buildings had designated fallout shelters.

And home shelters were advertised on television, radio, and in print media. Or, with a set of plans, you could build your own "protection." All you had to do is dig a hole, or find one already dug for you.

Not that any of these precautions would get you through the half-life of a nuclear conflagration. A logical extension of such survival strategies might be the world envisioned here by Galouye.

We can expect that of a science fiction writer, at least of a good one. They are expected to speculate to logical conclusions. And one of the most fascinating aspects of Galouye's post-nuclear reality is that the inability to see, at least visually, is not so much a handicap as it is a shift in emphasis to different senses. Humans often believe vision is the most important of the five senses. What if it became the least important?

If reality is to some degree a matter of perception, how does it change when we perceive the world through the senses other than vision?

And what of darkness? Jared can't find it although he is surrounded by it. And he believes in Light Almighty though he has never "seen" it.

But Jared believes that before he can understand Light Almighty, he must first find darkness.

Dark Universe reminds me of Edwin A. Abbot's *Flatland* in that it speculates about human sensory perception in a way similar to how Abbot explores spatial dimensions.

The plot of the novel is simple enough. Simple as an epic poem. Simple as a myth. It speaks to us now not through the particulars of its situations, but through the perplexities apparent in those situations. The objective existence of light and dark are not as important to Jared and his fellow humans here as the way in which these terms are defined.

It's that aspect of Jared's search that still speaks to us and makes *Dark Universe* more than an artifact of an age of nuclear paranoia. Not that we can't still be frightened by the threat of nuclear annihilation—the threat remains. But the fear goes further back, all the way to all our childhood fears and what they might represent. The monsters, after all, are to be found under the bed, one step up from the world below.

Galouye understood the enigma of darkness in its most primal manifestations.

We aren't necessarily frightened because we build bombs. We build bombs because we are frightened.

And though the greatest source of darkness may be found in the blinding flash of a nuclear explosion, it is only because of darkness that we can see the stars.

Richard Chwedyk is a Nebula Award-winning science fiction writer who has also been nominated for the Hugo, Sturgeon, and Rhysling awards. He also writes a book review column for Galaxy's Edge *magazine and teaches at Columbia College, Chicago.*

DARK UNIVERSE

CHAPTER ONE

PAUSING BESIDE THE HANGING NEEDLE of rock, Jared tapped it with his lance. Precise, staccato-like tones filled the passageway.

"Hear it?" he coaxed. "It's right up ahead."

"I don't hear a thing." Owen edged forward, stumbled and fell lightly against Jared's back. "Nothing but mud and hanging stones."

"No pits?"

"None that *I* can hear."

"There's one not twenty paces off. Better stick close to me."

Jared tapped the rock again, inclining an ear so he would miss none of the subtle echoes. There it was, all right—massive and evil as it clung to a nearby ledge listening to their advance.

Ahead were no more needles of rock he could conveniently tap. The last echoes had told him that much. So he produced a pair of clickstones from his pouch and brought them together sharply in the hollow of his hand, concentrating on the returning tones. To his right, his ears traced out great formations of rocks, folded one over the other and reflecting a confusing pattern of sound.

Owen clutched his shoulder as they pressed forward. "It's too smart. We'll never catch up with it."

"Of course we will. It'll get annoyed and attack sooner or later. Then there'll be one less soubat to contend with."

"But Radiation! It's pitch silent! I can't even hear where I'm going!"

"What do you think I'm using clickstones for?"

"I'm used to the central echo caster."

Jared laughed. "That's the trouble with you pre-Survivors. Depend too much on the familiar things."

Owen's sarcastic snort was justified. For Jared, at twenty-seven pregnancy periods of age, was not only his senior by less than two gestations, but also was still a pre-Survivor himself.

Drawing up beneath the ledge, Jared unslung his bow. Then he handed Owen the spear and stones. "Stay here and click out some distinct tones—about a pulse apart."

He eased forward, arrow strung. Now the ledge was casting back sharp echoes. The soubat was stirring, folding and unfolding its immense, leathery wings. He paused and listened to the evil form, audibly outlined against the smooth, rock background. Furry, oval face—twice as large as his own. Alert ears, cupped and pointed. Clenched talons, sharp as the jagged rocks to which they clung. And twin *pings* of reflected sound brought the impression of bared fangs.

"Is it still there?" Owen whispered anxiously.

"Can't you hear it yet?"

"No, but I can sure smell the thing. It—"

Abruptly the soubat released its grip and dropped.

Jared didn't need clickstones now. The furious flapping of wings was a direct, unmistakable target. He drew the bow, placing the feathered end of the arrow against his ear, and released the string.

The creature screamed—a piercing, ragged cry that reverberated in the passage.

"Good Light Almighty!" Owen exclaimed. "You got it!"

"Just punctured a wing." Jared reached for another arrow. *"Quick*—give me some more echoes!"

But it was too late. The thrashing of its wings was carrying the soubat off down a branch passage.

Listening to the retreating sound, Jared absently fingered his beard. Cropped close to his chin, it was a dense growth that projected bluntly forward, giving his face a self-confident tone. Taller than the span of a bowstring, he was lancelike in posture and his limbs were solidly corded. Although shoulder length in the back, his hair was trimmed in front, leaving ears unobstructed and face fully exposed. This accommodated his fondness for open eyes. It was a preference that wasn't based on religious belief, but rather on his dislike for the facial tautness which came with closed eyes.

Later, the side passage narrowed and received a river that flowed up out of the ground, leaving only a thin strip of slippery rock for them to tread.

Gripping his arm, Owen asked, "What's up ahead?"

Jared sounded the clickstones. "No low rocks. No pits. The stream flows off into the wall and the passage widens again."

He was listening more intently, though, to other, almost lost echoes—minor reflections from small things that slid into the river as they retreated from the disturbing noise of the stones.

"Make a note of this place," he said. "It's crawling with game."

"Salamanders?"

"Hundreds of them. That means decent-sized fish and hordes of crayfish."

Owen laughed. "I can just hear the Prime Survivor authorizing a hunting expedition *here*. Nobody's ever been *this* far before."

"*I* have."

"When?" the other asked skeptically.

They cleared the stream and were back on dry ground again.

"Eight or nine pregnancy periods ago."

"Radiation—but you were a child then! And you came *here*— *this* far from the Lower Level?"

"More than once."

"Why?"

"To hunt for something."

"What?"

"Darkness."

Owen chuckled. "You don't *find* Darkness. You *commit* it."

"So the Guardian says. He shouts, 'Darkness abounds in the worlds of men!' And he says that means sin and evil prevail. But I don't believe it means that."

"What *do* you believe?"

"Darkness must be something real. Only, we can't recognize it."

Again Owen laughed. "If you can't recognize it, then how do you expect to find it?"

Jared disregarded the other's skepticism. "There's a clue. We know that in the Original World—the first world that man inhabited after he left Paradise—we were closer to Light Almighty. In other words, it was a good world. Now let's suppose there's some sort of connection between sin and evil and this Darkness stuff. That means there must be *less* Darkness in the Original World. Right?"

"I suppose so."

"Then all I have to do is find something there's less of in the Original World."

Clickstone echoes traced out a massive obstruction ahead and Jared slowed his pace. He reached the barricade and explored it with his fingers. Rocks, piled one upon the other, stretched completely across the passage, rearing up to his shoulder.

"Here it is," he announced, "—the Barrier."

Owen's grip firmed on his arm. "*The* Barrier?"

"We can make it over the top easily."

"But—the law! We can't go past the Barrier!"

Jared dragged him along. "Come on. There are *no* monsters. Nothing to be afraid of—except maybe a soubat or two."

"But they say it's worse than Radiation itself!"

"That's what they *tell* you." By now Jared had him halfway up the mound. "They even say you'll find the Twin Devils Cobalt and Strontium waiting to carry you off to the depths of Radiation. Rot! Compost!"

"But the Punishment Pit!"

Scrambling down the other side, Jared rattled his clickstones with more than one purpose in mind. Besides drowning out Owen's protests, the clatter also plumbed the passage before them. Owen had somehow gotten in front and the close-quarter echoes were clearly transmitting sonic impressions of a stocky body, alert with tension and protected by outstretched, groping arms.

"For Light's sake!" Jared rebuked. "Get your hands down! I'll tell you if you're going to bump into anything."

The next echo crest caught the other's shrug. "So I'm no good with clickstones," he gruffed, stepping off in a resentful stride.

Jared followed, appreciating Owen's pluck. Cautious and hesitant, he took things reluctantly. But when the final *click* fetched its impression of an unavoidable situation with natural foe or Zivver, there wasn't a more determined fighter around.

Zivvers and soubats and bottomless pits, Jared reflected—those were the challenges of existence. If it weren't for them the Lower Level World and its passages would be as safe as Paradise itself was before man turned his back on Light Almighty and, as the legend had it, came to the various worlds that men and Zivvers now inhabited.

At the moment, though, only the soubats held his concern. One in particular—a vicious, marauding creature that had winged furiously into the Lower Level and snatched away a sheep.

He spat in disgust, recalling the venomous expletives his archery instructor had muttered long ago: "Stinking, Light damned things from the bowels of Radiation!"

"What *are* soubats?" one of the young archers had asked.

"They started off like the inoffensive little bats whose manure we collect for the plants. But they had truck with the Devils somewhere along the way. Either Cobalt or Strontium took one of them down to Radiation and made it over into a supercreature. From that one came all the soubats we have to contend with now."

Jared filled the passage with anxious, probing echoes. Owen, stubbornly maintaining the lead, was advancing more cautiously now, sending his feet out in sliding motions rather than pronounced steps.

The other's closed-eyes preference brought a smile to Jared's lips. It was a habit that would never be broken. It accommodated the belief that the eyes themselves should be protected and preserved for feeling the Great Light Almighty's presence on His Return.

But there wasn't anything objectionable about Owen, Jared assured himself, except that he was too susceptible to literal acceptance of the legends. Like the one which held that Light had resented man's invention of the manna plant and had cast him out of Paradise and into eternal Darkness, whatever that was.

One *click* and Owen was there—several paces ahead. Another and he was gone. In the interim there had been a distressed shout and the sound of flesh impacting on rock. Then:

"For Light's sake! Get me out of here!"

More echoes disclosed the presence of the shallow pit which had, until then, lurked in the echo void ahead of Owen.

Standing on the lip of the cavity, Jared lowered his lance. The other grabbed hold and started to pull himself out. But Jared tensed, wrenched the spear free and cast himself on the ground. He barely escaped clawing talons as the soubat swooped down.

"We're going to get a soubat!" he shouted exultantly.

By its shrieks, he tracked the animal as it made a ranging turn, gaining altitude, then dived down in a second, screaming attack. Jared lunged up, anchored the spear in a crevice and braced himself along the shaft, aiming it at the onrushing fury.

All Radiation broke loose as three hundred pounds of wrath hit Jared in a single, violent blast and bowled him over. He rose and felt the warmth of blood on his arm where talon had laid open flesh.

"Jared! You all right?"

"Stay down! It might come back!" He ran a hand over the ground and retrieved his bow.

But all was silent. The soubat had retreated once more, this time possibly with a spear wound added to its distress.

Owen climbed out of the pit. "You hurt?"

"Just a couple of scratches."

"Did you get it?"

"Radiation no! But I know where it is."

"I'm not even asking where. Let's go home."

Jared tapped the ground with his bow and listened. "It turned off into the Original World—up ahead."

"Let's go back, Jared!"

"Not until I get that thing's tusks in my pouch."

"You're going to get them *somewhere else!*"

14

But Jared went on. And, reluctantly, Owen followed.

Later he asked, "Are you *really* determined to find Darkness?"

"I'm going to find it if it takes the rest of my life."

"Why bother with hunting evil?"

"Because I'm really listening for something else. And Darkness may be just a step along the way."

"What *are* you hunting for?"

"Light."

"The Great Light Almighty," Owen reminded, reciting one of the tenets, "is present in the souls of good men and—"

"Suppose," Jared broke in boldly, "Light isn't God, but something else?"

The other's religious sensitivity was shocked. Jared could tell by his breathless silence, by the slight acceleration of his pulse.

"What else *could* Light Almighty be?" Owen asked finally.

"I don't know. But I'm sure it's something good. And if I can find it, life will be better for all mankind."

"What makes you think that?"

"If Darkness is connected with evil, and if Light is its opposite, then Light must be good. And if I find Darkness, then I may have some kind of idea as to the nature of Light."

Owen snorted. "That's ridiculous! You mean you think our beliefs are wrong?"

"Not altogether. Maybe just twisted around. You know what happens when a story passes from mouth to mouth. Just think what *could* happen to it passing from generation to generation."

Jared returned his attention to the passage as the clickstone echoes betrayed a great hollow space in the wall on his right.

They stood in the vaulted entrance to the Original World and Jared's *clicks* lost themselves in the silence of a vast expanse. He substituted his largest, hardest pair of sounding rocks. These he had to clap together with considerable force to produce reports loud enough to carry to the farthest recesses and back.

First—the soubat. Its lingering stench verified that the thing was somewhere in here. But none of the returning echoes carried with it the textural impression of leathery wings or soft, furry body.

"The soubat?" Owen asked anxiously.

"It's hiding," Jared said between *clicks*. Then, to take his friend's mind off the danger, "How good are you? What do you hear?"

"A Radiation of a big world."

"Right. Go on."

"In the space just ahead—softness. A clump or two of—"

"Manna plants. Growing close around a single hot spring. I can hear scores of empty pits too—pits where boiling water used to feed the energy hunger of *thousands* of plants. But, go ahead."

"Over there on the left, a pool—a big one."

"Good!" Jared complimented. "Fed by a stream. What else?"

"I—Radiation! Something queer. A lot of queer things."

Jared advanced. "Those are living quarters—stretched all around the wall."

"But I don't understand." Owen, confused, followed along. "They're out in the open!"

"When the people lived here they didn't have to find their privacy in grottoes. They *built* walls around spaces out in the open."

"*Square* walls?"

"They had a flair for geometry, I suppose."

Owen pulled back. "Let's get out of here! They say Radiation isn't too far from the Original World!"

"Maybe they say that just to keep us out."

"I'm beginning to think that you don't believe *anything*."

"Of course I do—whatever I can hear, feel, taste, or smell." Jared changed position and the echoes from his stones aligned themselves with an opening in one of the living quarters.

"Soubat!" he whispered as the stream of *clicks* brought back an impression of the thing hanging inside the cubicle. "You take the spear. We'll be ready for it this time!"

Cautiously, he approached within arrow range of the structure, securing his stones. He didn't need them now—not with the sound of the thing's breathing as clear as the snorting of an angry bull.

He strung an arrow and wedged a second under his belt where it would be within convenient reach. Behind him, he heard Owen dig the spear shaft into the ground. Then he asked, "Ready?"

"Let it fly," Owen urged. And there was no quaver in his voice. The last *click* had sounded. The lines were drawn.

Aiming at the hissing breath, he released the bowstring.

The arrow screamed through the air and thudded into something solid—too solid to be animal flesh. Screeching its rage, the soubat hurtled toward them. Jared strung the second arrow, taking his lead in advance of the winged fury.

He let it fly and ducked.

The beast shrieked in agony as it zipped by overhead. Then there was a *thud* and a final rush of air from the great lungs.

"For Light's sake!" came the familiar exclamation. "Get this stinking thing off me!"

Grinning, Jared tapped his bow on the solid rock underfoot and, in return, picked up the sonic effects of a disheveled heap— soubat, human, broken lance, and protruding arrow shaft.

Owen squirmed out finally. "Well, we got the damned thing. *Now* can we go home?"

"As soon as I finish." Jared was already cutting out the tusks.

Soubats and Zivvers. One by one, the Lower and Upper Level people could hope to eliminate the former. But what would prevail against the latter? What *could* prevail against creatures who used no clickstones but who, nevertheless, knew everything about their surroundings? It was an uncanny ability nobody could explain, except to say they were possessed of Cobalt or Strontium.

Oh, well, Jared mused, prophecy held that man would vanquish all his foes. He supposed that included the Zivvers also, although to him it had always seemed that Zivvers were human too—after a fashion.

He finished prying out the first tusk and some remote recess of his mind dredged up memories of childhood teachings:

What is Light?
Light is a Spirit.

Where is Light?
If it weren't for the evil in man, Light would be everywhere.
Can we feel or hear Light?
No, but in the hereafter we shall all see Him.

Rubbish! Anyway, no one could explain the word *see*. What did you do to the Almighty when you *seed* Him?

He secured the tusks in his pouch and stood up, listening all around. There was *something* here that there might be less of than in the other worlds—something man called "Darkness" and defined as sin and evil. But what was it?

"Jared, come here!"

He used clickstones to establish Owen's location. The echoes brought an impression of his friend standing by a thick pole that was leaning over at such an angle as to be almost lying on the ground. He was feeling an object dangling from the upthrust end—something round and brittle that hurled back distinct, ringing tones.

"It's a *Bulb!*" Owen exclaimed. "Just like the Guardian's relic of Light Almighty!"

Jared's memory resurrected more of the beliefs:

So compassionate was the Almighty (it was the Guardian of the Way's voice that came back now) *that when He banished man from Paradise, He sent parts of Himself to be with us for a while. And He dwelled in many little vessels like this Holy Bulb.*

There was a noise somewhere among the living quarters.

"Light!" Owen swore. "Do you smell *that?*"

Indeed Jared did smell it. It was so offensively alien that it made the hair bristle on his neck. He rattled his clickstones desperately, backing off all the while.

The echoes brought an incredible, jumbled pattern of sound—impressions of something human, but not human; unbelievably evil because it was different, yet arresting because it seemed to have a pair of arms and legs and a head and stood more or less upright. It was advancing, trying to take them by surprise.

Jared reached into his quiver. But there were no more arrows. Then, terrified, he cast his bow away and turned to flee.

"Oh, Light!" Owen moaned, scrambling back toward the exit. "What in Radiation *is* it?"

But Jared couldn't answer. He had all he could do trying to find the way out while keeping his ears on the unholy menace. It was reeking more terribly than a thousand soubats.

"It's Strontium himself!" Owen decided. "The legends are true! The Twin Devils *are* here!" He turned and bolted for the exit, his own bewildered shouts providing the guiding echoes.

Jared only stood there, paralyzed by a sensation altogether beyond comprehension. His auditory impression of the monstrous form was clear: it seemed the thing's entire body was made up of fluttering sheets of flesh. But there was something else—a vague yet vivid bridge of *noiseless* echoes that spanned the distance from the creature and boiled down into the depths of his conscious.

Sounds, odors, tastes, the pressure of the rocks and material things around him—all seemed to pour into his being, bringing pain. He clamped his hands over his face and raced after Owen.

A *zip-hiss* cleaved the air above his head and a moment later Owen's voice rose in a cry of anguished terror. Then Jared heard his friend collapse, falling at the entrance to the Original World.

He reached the spot where Owen lay, slung the unconscious form over his shoulder and plunged on.

Zip-hiss.

Something grazed his arm, leaving droplets of moisture clinging to the flesh. In the next instant he was tripping, falling, picking himself up and racing on under the burden of Owen's dead weight. And he was seized by a sudden grogginess he couldn't explain.

Deaf now, he staggered against the piled boulders that formed the passage's left wall and groped his way around one of the huge rocks. Then he stumbled into a crevice between two outcroppings and fell with Owen on top of him, lapsing into unconsciousness.

CHAPTER TWO

"GOOD LIGHT! LET'S GET OUT of here!"

Owen's whisper jarred him awake and Jared struggled erect. Then, remembering the Original World and its terror, he lurched back.

"It's gone now," the other assured.

"You certain?"

"Yes. I heard it listening all around out there. Then it left. What in Radiation was it—Cobalt? Strontium?"

Jared crawled from among the boulders and reached for a pair of clickstones. But then he thought better of making any noise.

Owen shuddered. "That smell! The sound of its shape!"

"And that other sensation!" Jared swore. "It was like something—psychic!"

He snapped his fingers softly, evaluating the reflected sounds, and continued around a great hanging stone that cascaded in graceful folds, flowing into a mound which strained up from the floor like a rearing giant.

"What other sensation?" Owen asked.

"Like all Radiation breaking loose in your head. Something that wasn't sound or smell or touch."

"I didn't hear anything like that."

"It wasn't hearing—I don't think."

"What made us pass out?"

"I don't know."

They went around a bend in the passage. Now that they had put some distance behind them, Jared began using his click-stones. "Light!" he exclaimed, relieved. "But I'd welcome even a soubat now!"

"Not without weapons you wouldn't."

And, as they crossed the Barrier and continued on alongside the wide river, Jared wondered why his friend hadn't experienced the same uncanny sensation he had. As far as he was concerned, that phase of the incident was even more frightening than the monster itself.

Then his lips grew grimly taut as an alarming possibility suggested itself: Suppose his Original World experience had been a punishment from the Great Almighty for his blasphemous belief that Light was something less than God?

They headed into more familiar territory and he announced, "We've got to report this to the Prime Survivor."

"We can't!" Owen protested. "We broke the law in coming here!"

Which was a complication Jared hadn't considered. Owen, to be sure, was in enough trouble as it was, having let the cattle get in the manna orchard last period.

Several hundred breaths later, Jared led the way around the final major hazard—a huge pit without bottom. He put his pebbles away. Not long afterward he hissed for silence, then drew Owen over to a recess in the wall.

"What's wrong?" the other demanded.

"Zivvers!" he whispered.

"I don't hear anything."

"You will in a few heartbeats. They're going down the Main Passage ahead. If they turn this way we may have to run for it."

The sounds in the other tunnel were more audible now. A sheep bleated and Jared recognized the pitch. "That's one of *our* animals. They raided the *Lower* Level."

The Zivver voices reached maximum volume as the pillagers passed the corridor intersection, then fell off.

"Come on," Jared urged. "They can't ziv us now."

He went not more than thirty paces, however, before he drew up and cautioned in his lowest voice, "Quiet!"

He held his breath and listened. Besides his own pounding heartbeat and Owen's fainter one, there was yet a third—not too far away, weak, but pumping violently with fright.

"What is it?" Owen asked.

"A Zivver."

"You're just getting the scent from that raiding party."

But Jared edged forward, weighing the auditory impressions, sniffing out other clues. The scent of the Zivver was unmistakable, but it was of minor proportions—that of a child! He drew in another whiff and detained it in his nasal chamber.

A girl Zivver!

Her heartbeat was distinct as he clicked his pebbles once to sound out the details of the cleft in which she was hiding. She stiffened at the noise, but didn't try to escape. Instead, she started crying—plaintively.

Owen relaxed. "It's only a child!"

"What's the matter?" Jared asked solicitously, but got no reply.

"What are you doing out here?" Owen tried.

"We're not going to hurt you," Jared promised. "What's wrong?"

"I—I can't ziv," she finally managed between sobs.

Jared knelt beside her. "You're a Zivver, aren't you?"

"Yes. I mean—no, I'm not. That is—"

She was perhaps thirteen gestations old. No older, certainly.

He led her out into the passageway. "Now—what's your name?"

"Estel."

"And why are you hiding out here, Estel?"

"I heard Mogan and the others coming. I ran in here so they wouldn't ziv me."

"Why don't you want them to find you?"

"So they won't take me back to the Zivver World."

"But that's where you belong, isn't it?"

She sniffled and Jared heard her wiping her cheeks dry.

"No," she said despondently. "Everybody there can ziv except me. And when I'm ready to become a Survivoress there won't be any Zivver Survivors who'll want me."

She began sobbing again. "I want to go to your world."

"You can't Estel," Owen tried to explain. "You don't understand what the sentiment is against—I mean—oh, you tell her, Jared."

Jared brushed the hair off her face when the reflection of his voice told him it was hanging there. "Once in the Lower Level we had a little girl—just about your age. She was sad because she couldn't hear. She wanted to run away. Then, one period, all of a sudden she could hear! And she was glad she had been smart enough *not* to run away and get lost before then."

"She was a Different One, wasn't she?" the girl asked.

"No. That's just the point. We only *thought* she was Different. And if she'd run away we never would have found out she wasn't."

Estel was silent as Jared led her toward the Main Passage.

"You mean," she asked after a while, "you think *I* might start *zivving?*"

He laughed and halted in the larger corridor beside a gurgling hot spring that sent its moist warmth swirling all around them. "I'm sure you'll start zivving—when you least expect it. And you'll be just as happy as that other little girl."

He listened in the direction of the Zivver raiders and readily picked up the sound of their receding voices. "What do you say, Estel—want to go home?"

"Well, all right—if you say so."

"Good girl!" He gave her a pat and propelled her in the direction of the other Zivvers. Then he cupped his hands and filled the passage with his voice. "There's one of your children back here!"

Owen shifted nervously. "Let's get out of here before we get stomped."

But Jared only laughed softly. "We'll be safe long enough to make sure they pick her up." He listened to the girl groping toward the returning Zivvers. "Anyway, they can't ziv us now."

"Why not?"

"We're standing right by this hot spring. They can't ziv anything too close to a boiling pit. That's something I learned on my own, gestations ago."

"What's a hot spring got to do with it?"

"I don't know. But it works."

"Well, if they can't ziv us, then they'll hear us."

"Point Number Two about Zivvers: they rely too much on zivving. Can't hear or smell worth a damned."

Soon they reached the entrance to the Lower Level World. Jared listened to Owen strike off for his own quarters, then he headed toward the Administration Grotto. He had made up his mind to report the Original World menace without implicating his friend.

Everything seemed normal—too normal, considering that Zivvers had just staged a raid. But then, the attacks were not so infrequent that the Survivors couldn't take them in stride when they did come.

Off to his left he caught Randel's scent and traced his climb up the pole to rewind the echo caster's pulley. Presently there was a speed-up in the mechanical *clacking* of the stones. And Jared listened to the more complete impressions the accelerated echoes provided. He made out the details of a work party spreading compost in the manna orchard, another digging out a new public grotto. Against the distant wall women were washing clothes in the river.

What struck him most, though, was the relative silence, which testified that *something* had happened. Even the children were drawn into small, voiceless clusters in front of the residential recesses.

There was a groan on his right—from the Injury Treatment Grotto—and he altered course. The central caster's reflected *clacks* told him someone was in front of the entrance. When he got closer he heard the feminine outline of Zelda.

"Trouble?" he asked.

"Zivvers," she said tersely. "Where were you?"

"Out after a soubat. Any casualties?"

"Alban and Survivor Bridley. Just roughed up though." Her voice filtered through hair that protectively draped her face.

"Any *Zivvers* get hurt?"

She laughed—a bitter outburst, like the twang of a bowstring. "You kidding? The Prime Survivor's been listening for you."

"Where is he?"

"Meeting with the Elders."

Jared continued on over to the Administration Grotto, but quieted his steps as he neared the entrance. Elder Haverty had the floor. His high-pitched, faltering voice was easily recognizable.

"We'll close up the entrance!" Haverty pounded the slab. "Then we won't have to worry about either the Zivvers *or* the soubats!"

"Sit down, Elder," came the authoritative voice of the Prime Survivor. "You're not making sense."

"Eh? How so?"

"We're told that was tried long ago. It only choked off the circulation and ran the heat up into the sweltering range."

"Least we could do," Haverty persisted, "is close it up *some*."

"Ought to be bigger as it is."

Jared eased up to the grotto entrance, but stood to one side so he wouldn't block any of the direct sounds from the caster. That would betray his presence even to the most insensitive ears.

The Prime Survivor was absently tapping the meeting slab with his fingernail, producing unobtrusive echoes.

"However," he said, "there *is* something we can do."

"Eh? What's that?" Elder Haverty asked.

"We couldn't do it by ourselves. It's too big a project. But we might undertake it as a joint enterprise with the Upper Level."

"We never had any joint enterprises with them before." It was Elder Maxwell's voice that entered the discussion.

"No, but they know we're going to have to pool our resources."

"What's the pitch?" asked Haverty.

"There's one *passageway* we might seal off. It wouldn't disturb the circulation in either the Upper or Lower Level. But, still, it would block us off from the Zivver World, as far as we know."

"The Main Passage," Maxwell guessed.

"Right. It'd be quite a job. But with both Levels working at it, we could do it in maybe half a pregnancy period."

"What about the Zivvers?" Haverty wanted to know. "Won't *they* have anything to say about that?"

Jared heard the Prime Survivor shrug his shoulders before continuing: "The two Levels far outnumber the Zivvers. We could keep adding material to this side of the barricade faster than they could haul it away from the other side. Eventually they'd give up."

Silence around the slab.

"Sounds good," Maxwell said. "Now all we got to do is sell the Upper Level on the idea."

"I think we can do that." The Prime Survivor cleared his throat. "Jared, come on in. We've been waiting for you."

The Prime Survivor might be getting old, Jared conceded, entering. But his ears and nose hadn't aged any. From the uninterrupted fingernail tapping, Jared received a composite impression of all the faces at the slab turned in his direction. There was a figure standing behind the Prime Survivor, he sensed.

The man moved into the clear and Jared picked up his features—short and somewhat stooped despite the comparative youthfulness his breathing suggested; hair flowing down past his forehead and around the sides of his face, with irregular openings to accommodate his ears and nose-mouth region. The fullest fuzzy-face in the Lower Level—Romel Fenton-Spur, his brother.

After the amenity of Reasonable Time for Recognition and Reflection had been observed, the Prime Survivor cleared his throat. "Jared, it's about time to apply for your Survivorship, don't you think?"

Jared's impulse was to brush aside the prosaic matter and launch into his revelation of the menace lurking in the Original World. But his presentation would have to be rational, so he decided to put it off a while. "I suppose so."

"Ever think of Unification?"

"Radiation no!" Then he pinched his tongue. "No, I haven't given it any thought."

"You realize, of course, that every man must become a Survivor and that the principal obligation of a Survivor is to survive."

"That's what I've been told."

"And surviving doesn't mean merely preserving your own life, but also passing it down through the generations."

"I'm aware of that."

"And you've found no one with whom you'd like to Unify?"

There was Zelda; but she was a fuzzy-face. There was Luise, who was both open-eyed and bare-faced to the clickstones. But she was always tittering. "No, Your Survivorship."

Romel snickered in anticipation of something or other and reproachful gestures were audible around the slab. For Jared, the sardonic giggle was reminiscent of earlier days when Romel's malicious pranks usually took the form of a swish-rope that would lash out from behind a boulder, twine around his ankles and snatch him off his feet. The fraternal antagonism was still there. Only, now it managed to find other adult—well, almost adult—forms of expression.

"Good!" the Prime Survivor enthused, rising. "I think we've found a Unification partner for you."

Jared sputtered a moment, then shed his respect with an oath. "Not for *me* you haven't!"

How could he tell them he had no time for Unification? That he had to be free to continue what he had started out to do long pregnancy periods ago? That he doubted their religious beliefs? That he wanted to spend his life proving Light was something physical, attainable in this existence—not something restricted to the afterlife?

Romel laughed and said, "That's for the Elders to decide."

"You're no Elder!"

"Neither are you. And, Jared, you're forgetting the Eminence of Seniority Code."

"To Radiation with the code!"

"That'll be enough," interrupted the Prime Survivor. "As Romel suggests, your Unification is for us to decide. Elders?"

Maxwell proposed, "Let's hear more about this arrangement first."

"Very well," the Prime Survivor went on. "Neither I nor the Wheel have let this get out yet, but we're both sold on the idea of joining hands between the two worlds. The Wheel thinks that end can be helped along by Unification between Jared and his niece."

"I won't do it!" Jared vowed. "The Wheel's just trying to pass off some spook of a relative!"

"Have you ever heard her?" the Prime Survivor asked.

"No! Have you?"

"No, but the Wheel says—"

"I don't care *what* the Wheel says!"

Jared drew back and listened. The Elders were rumbling impatiently. They weren't too happy over his stubbornness. If he didn't do something—*anything*—soon, they'd have him hooked!

"There's a monster in the Original World," he blurted, "I was out chasing a soubat and—"

"The Original World?" asked Elder Maxwell incredulously.

"Yes! And this thing—it reeked like Radiation and—"

"Do you realize what you've done?" the Prime Survivor demanded severely. "Crossing the Barrier is the worst possible offense, besides Murder and Misplacement of Bulky Objects!"

"But this creature! I'm trying to tell you I heard something *evil!*"

The Prime Survivor's voice drowned out even the central caster's *clacks.* "What in the name of Light Almighty did you *expect* to find in the Original World? Why do you think we have laws, the Barrier?"

"This calls for severe punishment," Romel suggested.

"You keep out of it!" snapped the Prime Survivor.

"The Punishment Pit?" Maxwell prompted.

"Eh? What?" clipped Haverty. "I imagine not. Not with a Unification arrangement pending."

Jared tried again. "This thing—it—"

"How about Seven Activity Periods of Detachment and Servility?" Haverty went on. "If he does it again—two gestations in the Pit."

"Lenient enough," Maxwell agreed. But he left unexpressed the general knowledge that only one prisoner had ever spent more than ten activity periods in the Pit and that he had had to be tied down for a whole gestation before he became harmless.

The Prime Survivor spoke up. "We'll make Jared's token punishment contingent on his accepting Unification."

The Elders eagerly smote the slab in approval.

"While serving your sentence," the Prime Survivor told Jared, "you can condition yourself for a visit to the Upper Level for the Five Periods Preparatory to Declaration of Unification Intentions."

Still snickering, Romel Fenton-Spur followed the Elders out.

When they were alone, Jared told the Prime Survivor, "That was a Radiation of a trick to play on *your own son!*"

The elder Fenton gave an expressionless shrug.

"Why tie in with that bunch up there?" Jared went on querulously. "We've fought Zivvers on our own this long, haven't we?"

"But they're multiplying, outgrowing their food supply."

"We'll set traps! We'll produce more food!"

Jared listened to the other shaking his head dourly. "On the contrary. We're going to produce *less*. You forget those three hot springs that dried up not thirty periods ago. That means dead manna plants—not as much food for the animals and ourselves."

Jared felt a touch of concern for the Prime Survivor. They were standing in the entrance to the grotto now and the sounds his father was reflecting conveyed their impressions of thinning limbs that had reluctantly yielded ample muscular development of a more active era. His hair was thin, but still swept proudly back over his head, evidencing an obstinate rejection of facial protection.

"It didn't have to be me," Jared grumbled. "Why not Romel?"

"He's a spur."

Jared didn't understand why the accident of illegitimate birth should make any difference in this situation. But he let the point go. "Well, anybody else then! There's Randel and Many and—"

"The Wheel and I have been discussing closer relations since you were hip high. And I've been building *you* up in his estimation until he thinks you're almost the equal of a Zivver."

Silence was perhaps the severest penalty of Jared's punishment. Silence and drudgery.

Hauling manure from the world of the small bats, trudging to the cricket domain to collect insect bodies as compost for the manna orchard. Rechanneling overflow from the boiling pits and getting steam-shriveled flesh in the process. Tending livestock and hand-feeding chicks until they could feel around for their own food.

And all the while never to be allowed a word. Never a word spoken to him except in direction-giving. No clickstones for fine hearing. Completely isolated from contact with others.

The first period lasted an eternity; the second, a dozen. The third he spent tending the orchard and consigning to Radiation everyone who approached because they came only to give orders—all but one.

That was Owen, who relayed instructions to begin excavating a public grotto. And Jared heard the troubled lines on his face. "If you think you ought to be working alongside me," Jared said, violating Vocal Detachment, "you'd better forget it. I *made* you cross the Barrier."

"I've been worrying about that too," Owen admitted distantly. "But not nearly as much as about something else."

"What?" Jared spread more compost around the manna plant stalk.

"I'm not worthy of being a Survivor. Not after the way I acted out there in the Original World."

"Forget the Original World."

"I can't." Owen's voice was filled with self-reproach as he moved off. "Whatever courage I had I left beyond the Barrier."

"Damned fool!" Jared called softly. "Keep away from there!"

He spent the fourth period languishing in solitude, without even a single person bringing instructions. The fifth he tried congratulating himself on at least having escaped the Pit. But throughout the sixth, as he bemoaned aching muscles and insufferable fatigue, he realized he might as well have gotten the more severe punishment. And before the final stint of exhausting drudgery ended, he wished to Radiation he *had* been sentenced to the Pit!

He finished wresting a final slab into place for one of the new grottoes, then pegged the echo caster into silence for the sleep period. Numb with weariness, he dragged himself to the Fenton recess.

Romel was asleep, but the Prime Survivor was still lying awake. "I'm glad it's over, son," he comforted. "Now get some rest. Tomorrow you'll be escorted to the Upper Level for the Five Periods Preparatory to Declaration of Unification Intentions."

Lacking strength to argue, Jared collapsed on his ledge.

"There's something you ought to know," his father went on soberly. "The Zivvers may be taking captives again. Owen went out to collect mushrooms four periods ago. He hasn't been heard from since."

Suddenly wide awake, Jared wasn't as exhausted as he had imagined. When the Prime Survivor fell asleep, he retrieved his clickstones and stole out of the Lower Level World, tempering condemnation of Owen's addle-headed pride with concern for his safety.

Fighting the impulse to drop in his tracks and sleep there forever, he pushed on past the place where he had encountered the Zivver child, along the bank beside the swift stream and into the smaller tunnel. Sounding the depths of each pit along the way, he reached the Barrier and dragged himself over it. On the other side his foot brushed across something familiar—Owen's quiver!

Beside it were a broken lance and two arrows. The bow, his clickstones told him, lay against the wall, cracked almost in half. Sniffing what might have been the lingering scent of the Original World creature, he backed off toward the Barrier.

Owen didn't even have a chance to use his weapons.

CHAPTER THREE

AT THE ENTRANCE TO THE Upper Level, the unfamiliar tones of the central echo caster brought Jared crude impressions of a world much like his own, with grottoes, activity areas, and livestock compounds. In addition it had a natural ledge running along the right wall and sloping down to the ground nearby.

Waiting for his reception escort, he turned his thoughts grimly back to the discovery of Owen's weapons on the other side of the Barrier. All he could think of then was that the evil creature had been a punishment sent by Light Himself for his sacrilegious rejection of established beliefs. Certainly he had been wrong. The Barrier *had*, after all, been erected solely to protect man from monster. Yet, he knew he would not forfeit his quest for Darkness. Nor would he let the uncertainty surrounding Owen's fate rest for very long.

"Jared Fenton?"

The voice, coming from behind a boulder on his left, took him by surprise. Stepping out into the full sound of the central caster, the man said. "I'm Lorenz, Adviser to Wheel Anselm."

Lorenz's voice suggested a person of short stature, small lung capacity, depressed chest. Added to this composite was the indirect sonic impression of a face whose audible features were rough with creases and lacked the soft, moist prominences of exposed eyeballs.

"Ten Touches of Familiarization?" Jared offered formally.

But the Adviser declined. "My faculties are adequate. I never forget audible effects." He struck off down a path that coursed through the hot-springs area.

Jared followed. "The Wheel expecting me?" Which was an unnecessary question, since a runner had come ahead.

"I wouldn't be out here to meet you if he wasn't."

Detecting hostility in the Adviser's blunt responses, Jared turned his attention fully on the man. The caster's tones were being harshly modulated by his expression of resentful determination.

"You don't want me up here, do you?" Jared asked frankly.

"I've advised against it. I don't hear where we can gain anything through close association with your world."

The Adviser's sullen attitude puzzled him for a moment—until he realized unification between the Upper and Lower Level would certainly affect Lorenz's established status.

The well-worn path had straightened and was now taking them along the right wall. Residential recesses cast back muffled gaps in the reflected sound pattern. And Jared sensed rather than clearly heard the knots of inquisitive people who were listening to him pass.

Presently the Adviser caught his shoulders and spun him to the right. "This is the Wheel's grotto."

Jared hesitated, getting his bearings. The recess was a deep one with many storage shelves. In the space before the entrance there was a large slab with adequate leg room carved in its sides. From its surface came the symmetrical sounds of empty manna shell bowls, giving the overall impression of an orderly arrangement for a meal that would accommodate many persons.

"Welcome to the Upper Level! I'm Noris Anselm, the Wheel."

Jared listened to his more than amply proportioned host advance around the slab with arm extended. That the hand found his on first thrust spoke well for the Wheel's perceptive ability.

"I've heard a lot about you, my boy!" He pumped Jared's arm. "Ten Touches?"

"Of course." Jared submitted to exploring fingers that swept methodically across his face and chest and along his arms.

"Well," said Anselm approvingly. "Clean-cut features—erect posture—agility—strength. I don't guess the Prime Survivor exaggerated too much. Feel away."

Jared's hands Familiarized themselves with a stout but not flaccid physique. Absence of a chest cloth, clipped hair and beard, suggested resistance to the aging process. And lids that flicked their protest to his touch signified abiding rejection of closed eyes.

Anselm laughed. "So you've come with Declaration of Unification Intentions in mind?" He led Jared to a bench beside the slab.

"Yes. The Prime Survivor says—"

"Ah—Prime Survivor Fenton. Haven't heard him in some time."

"He sends—"

"Good old Evan!" the Wheel declared expansively. "He's got a likely idea—wanting the two Levels closer. What do you think?"

"At first I—"

"Of course you do. It doesn't take much imagination to hear the advantages, does it?"

Abandoning hope of completing a sentence, Jared accepted the question as rhetorical while he concentrated on faint impressions coming from the mouth of the grotto behind him. Someone had moved out into the entrance and was silently listening on. Reflected *clacks* fetched the outline of a youthful, feminine form.

"I said," Anselm repeated, "it doesn't take much imagination to hear the benefits of uniting the Levels."

Jared drew attentively erect. "Not at all. The Prime Survivor says there's a lot to be gained. He—"

"About this Unification. Figure you're ready for it?"

At least Jared had managed to finish *one* answer. But there was no point in pushing his success, so he simply said, "Yes."

"Good boy! Della's going to make a fine Survivoress. A little headstrong, perhaps. But you take my own Unification ..."

The Wheel embarked on a lengthy dissertation while Jared's attention went back to the furtive girl. At least he knew who she was. At the mention of the name "Della," her breathing had faltered and he had heard a subjective quickening of her pulse.

The brisk, clear tones of the Wheel's voice produced sharp-sounding echoes. And Jared took note of the girl's precise, smooth profile. High cheekbones accentuated the self-confident tilt of her chin. Her eyes were wide open and her hair was arranged in a style he hadn't heard before. Swept tightly away from her face, it was banded in the back and went streaming bushily down her spine. His imagination provided him with a pleasing echo composite of Della racing down a windy passageway, long tresses fluttering behind.

"... But Lydia and I never had a son." His garrulous host had gone on to another subject by now. "Still, I think it would be best if the Wheelship remained in the Anselm line, don't you?"

"To be sure." Jared had lost track of the conversation.

"And the only way that can come about without complications is through Unification between you and my niece."

This, Jared reasoned, should be the cue for the girl to step from concealment. But she didn't budge.

The Upper Level had recovered from his arrival and now he listened to the sounds of a normal world—children shouting at play, women grotto-cleaning, men busy at their chores, a game of clatterball in progress on the field beyond the livestock pens.

The Wheel gripped his arm and said, "Well, we'll get better acquainted later on. There'll be a formal dinner this period where you'll Familiarize yourself with Della. But, first, I've had a recess prepared for your convenience."

Jared was led off along the row of residential grottoes. But they hadn't gone far when he was drawn to a halt.

"The Prime Survivor says you have a remarkable pair of ears, my boy. Let's hear how good they are."

Somewhat embarrassed, Jared turned his attention to the things about him. After a moment his ears were drawn to the ridge running along the far wall.

"I hear something on that ledge," he said. "There's a boy lying up there listening out over the world."

Anselm drew in a surprised breath. Then he shouted, "Myra, your child up on that shelf again?"

A woman nearby called out, "Timmy! Timmy, where are you?"

And a slight, remote voice answered, "Up here, Mother."
"Incredible!" exclaimed the Wheel. "Utterly incredible!"

As the formal dinner neared its end, Anselm thudded his drinking shell down on the slab and assured the other guests, "It was quite remarkable! There was the lad, *all the way across the world.* But Jared heard him anyway. How'd you do it, my boy?"

Jared would have let the matter drop. He'd had his fill of uneasiness, each guest having taken the full Ten Touches.

"There's a smooth dome behind the ledge," he explained wearily. "It magnifies the tones from the central caster."

"Nonsense, my boy! It was an amazing feat!"

The slab came alive with murmurs of respect.

Adviser Lorenz laughed. "Listening to the Wheel tell about it, I'd almost suspect our visitor might be a Zivver."

An uncomfortable hush followed. Jared could hear the Adviser's complacent smile. "It was remarkable," Anselm insisted.

There was a lull in the conversation and Jared steered the talk away from himself. "I enjoyed the crayfish, but the salamander was especially good. I've never tasted anything like it before."

"Indeed you haven't," Anselm boasted. "And we have Survivoress Bates to thank. Tell our guest how you manage it, Survivoress."

A stout woman across the slab said, "I had an idea meat would taste better if we could get away from soaking it directly in boiling water. So we tried putting the cuts in watertight shells and sinking them in the hot springs. This way the meat's *dry* cooked."

On the edge of his hearing, Jared sensed that Della was listening to his slight movements.

"The Survivoress used to prepare salamander even better," offered Lorenz.

"When we still had the big boiling pit," the woman said.

"When you *still* had it?" Jared asked, interested.

"It dried up a while back, along with a couple of others," Anselm explained. "But I suppose we'll be able to do without them."

The other guests had begun drifting off toward their grottoes—all except Della. But still she ignored Jared.

The Wheel gripped his shoulder, whispered "Good luck, my boy!" and headed for his own recess.

Someone turned off the echo caster, ending the activity period, and Jared sat listening to the girl's even breathing. He casually tapped the slab with a fingernail and studied the reflected impressions of a creased feminine brow and full lips compressed with concern.

He moved closer. "Ten Touches?"

There was a sharp alteration in the sound pattern as she faced the other way. But she offered no protest to Familiarization.

His probing fingers traced out her profile first, then verified the firmness of her cheekbones. He explored further the odd hair style and her level shoulders. The skin there was warm and full, its smoothness harshly broken by the overlay of halter straps.

She drew back. "I'm sure you'll recognize me the next time."

If he was going to be stuck with Unification, Jared decided, he could fare worse by way of a partner.

He waited for the feel of her fingers. But none came. Instead, she slid off the bench and walked casually toward a natural grotto whose emptiness reflected her footfalls. He followed.

"How does it feel," she asked finally, "to have Unification forced on you?" Her words bore more than a trace of bitter indignation.

"I don't much care for it."

"Then why don't you refuse?" She sat on a ledge in the grotto.

He paused outside, tracing the details of the recess as relayed by her rebounding words. "Why don't *you?*"

"I don't have much of a choice. The Wheel's made up his mind."

"That's tough." Her attitude suggested that the whole arrangement was his idea. But he supposed she did have a right to be indignant. So he added, "I guess we could both do worse."

"Maybe *you* could. But I might have my pick of a dozen Upper Level men I'd prefer."

He bristled. "How do you know? You haven't even had Ten Touches."

She scooped up a stone and tossed it. *Kerplunk.*

"I didn't ask for them," she said. "And I don't want them."

He wondered whether a few swats in the right place wouldn't soften her tongue. "I'm not *that* objectionable!"

"You—objectionable? Paradise no!" she returned. "You're *Jared Fenton* of the Lower Level!"

Another pebble went *kerplunk*.

"'I hear something on that ledge,'" she mocked his earlier words. "'There's a boy lying up there listening out over the world.'"

Della threw several more stones while he stood there with his ears trained severely on her. They all went *kerplunk*.

"That demonstration was your uncle's idea," he reminded her.

Instead of answering, she continued tossing rocks into the water. She had him on the defensive. And if he chose to strike back it would only seem he was in favor of their Unification, which couldn't be further from the truth. Unification and the obligations it brought would mean an end to his search for Light.

Della rose and went to the grotto wall where a group of slender stones hung needlelike from the ceiling. She stroked them lightly, and melodious tones filled the recess with vibrant softness. It was a wistful tune that sang of pleasant things with deep, tender meaning. He was stirred by the girl's sensitive talent as he was by the sharp contrasts the music showed in her nature.

She slapped several of the stones in an impulsive burst of temperament, then scooped up another pebble. Whispering through the air, her arm arched out to toss the rock as she turned and strode defiantly from the grotto.

Kerplunk.

Curious, he went over to explore for the puddle. He was concerned over the fact that he hadn't detected the liquid softness of water in the recess. He found the pool a moment later, however. A deep, almost still spring, it had a surface area no larger than his palm.

Yet, over a distance of thirty paces, Della had casually cast more than a dozen stones—detecting and hitting her target with each one!

Through much of the ceremony the next period, Jared found his thoughts returning to the girl. He wasn't as much disturbed by her arrogance as he was by the possibility that her pebble-throwing demonstration may have been calculated. Was she merely belittling his ability? Or was the performance really as casual as it had seemed? In either case, the capacity itself remained unexplained.

Wheel Anselm moved closer to him on the Bench of Honor and slapped his back. "That Drake's plenty good, don't you think?"

Jared had to agree, although there were several Lower Level Survivors who could hit more than three out of nine arrow targets.

He concentrated on the reflected *clacks* of the central caster and listened to Drake draw another arrow. An anxious silence fell over the gallery and Jared tried unsuccessfully to pick out Della's breathing and heartbeat.

Drake's bowstring *twanged* and the arrow whistled across the range. But the muffled *thud* of its impact revealed that it had missed the target and dug into earth.

After a moment the Official Scorer called out, "Two hand widths to the right. Score: three out of ten."

There was a burst of applause.

"Good, isn't he?" Anselm boasted.

Jared became more aware of Lorenz's breathing as the Adviser turned toward him and said, "I should think you'd be eager to get in on these contests."

Still smarting from Della's insinuation that he was conceited, Jared said noncommittally, "I'm prepared for anything."

The Wheel overheard and exclaimed, "That's fine, my boy!" He rose and announced, "Our visitor's going to lead off the spear-throwing competition!"

More applause. Jared wondered, though, whether he had detected a feminine breath escaping in contempt.

Lorenz brought him over to the spear rack and he spent some time selecting his lances.

"What's the target?" he asked.

"Woven husk discs—two hand spans wide—at fifty paces." The Adviser caught his arm and pointed it. "They're against that bank."

"I can hear them," Jared assured. "But I want *my* targets thrown up in the air."

Lorenz drew back. "You must want to hear how big a fool you can make of yourself."

"It's my party." Jared gathered up his spears. "You just toss the discs."

So Della was certain he had an exaggerated opinion of himself, was she? Riled, he broke out his clickstones and retreated to the fringe of the hot-springs area. Then he began a steady, brisk beat with the pebbles in his left hand. The familiar, refined tones supplemented those of the echo caster. And now he could clearly hear the things about him—the ledge on his right, the hollowness of the passageway behind him, Lorenz standing ready to cast the discs.

"Target up!" he shouted at the Adviser.

The first manna husk disc *swished* through the air and he let a spear fly. Wicker crunched under the impact of pointed shaft, then disc and lance clattered to the ground together.

Momentarily, he sensed something was out of place. But he couldn't decide what it was. "Target up!"

Another direct hit. And then another.

Exclamations from the gallery distracted him and he missed his fourth shot. He waited for silence before ordering more discs into the air. The next five shots found their mark. Then he paused and listened intensely around him. Somehow he couldn't ignore the vague suspicion that something wasn't as it should be.

"That was the last target," the Adviser shouted. "Get another," Jared called back, letting his remaining spear lie on the ground.

An awed silence hung over the gallery. Then Anselm laughed and bellowed, "By Light! Eight out of nine!"

"With *that* kind of ability," Lorenz added from the distance, "he *must* be a Zivver."

Jared spun around. That was it—*Zivvers!* He realized that for heartbeats now he had been catching their scent!

Just then someone shouted, "Zivvers! Up on the ledge!"

Disorder swept the world. Women screamed and scrambled for their children while Survivors bolted for the weapons rack.

Jared heard a spear *zip* down from the height and clatter against the Bench of Honor. The Wheel swore apprehensively.

"Everybody stay where you are!" boomed a voice Jared had not forgotten from previous raids—that of Mogan, the Zivver leader. "Or the Wheel gets a shaft in the chest!"

By now Jared had pieced together a more or less complete auditory composite of the situation. Mogan and a score of Zivvers were spaced along the ledge, the central caster's tones rebounding clearly against their raised lances. A lone Zivver guarded the entrance, standing next to the large boulder.

As gingerly as he could, Jared stooped to retrieve his spear. But a lance *hissed* down and stabbed into the ground in front of him.

"I said *nobody* moves!" Mogan's menacing voice poured down.

Even if he could get his hand on the spear, Jared realized, the ledge would be out of range. The rear guard at the entrance, however, was a different matter. And there was nothing but boiling pits and manna plants between him and the man. If he could make it to the first spring, none of the raiders would be able to ziv his progress through the heated area.

He traced the flight of another spear from the ledge. It sank into the echo caster's shaft, wedging itself against the pulley. And the Upper Level was thrown into stark silence.

"Take what you want," the Wheel quavered, "and leave us alone."

Jared sidled toward the first hot spring.

"What do you know about a Zivver who's been missing for the past twenty periods?" Mogan demanded.

"Nothing at all!" Anselm assured him.

"Like Radiation you don't! But we'll find out for ourselves before we leave."

Moist warmth swirled against Jared's chest and he lunged the rest of the way into the vapors.

"We don't know anything about it!" the Wheel reiterated. "We've had a Survivor missing too—for over fifty periods!"

Clicking his teeth faintly to produce echoes as he crept through the hot-springs area, Jared pulled up sharply. A Zivver missing? One of the Upper Level men too? Could there be any connection between those two occurrences and what had happened to Owen? Had the Original World monster crossed the Barrier after all?

Mogan barked, "Norton, Sellers—go search their grottoes!"

Jared cleared the last boiling pit and stepped soundlessly over to the boulder. Now only the big rock stood between him and the raider guarding the entrance. And the man's breathing and heartbeat clearly divulged his exact location. No one had ever enjoyed such an advantage of potential surprise over a lone Zivver! But he had to strike fast. Norton and Sellers were already trotting down the incline and would, in the next three or four breaths, pass within a few paces of the boulder.

More things than he could keep track of happened in the next instant. Even as he started his lunge around the rock, he caught the horrible stench of the thing from the Original World. It was too late, however, to check his charge.

Then, as he broke around the boulder, a great cone of roaring silence screamed out of the passageway. The incredible sensation struck him squarely in the face with deafening force. It was as though obscure regions were being opened in his mind—as though thousands of sensitive nerves that had never been stimulated before were suddenly flooding his brain with alien impulses.

In that same instant he heard the *zip-hiss* that had sounded in the Original World just before Owen collapsed. And he listened first to the Zivver crumpling before him and then to the frantic cries of distress rising from his rear.

Whirling to flee before the monster and the terrifying noise that he could neither hear nor feel, Jared was only vaguely aware of the Zivver spear that was screeching in his direction.

He tried to duck at the last heartbeat.

But he was too late.

CHAPTER FOUR

GUIDED BY CLICKSTONES, JARED WENT cautiously down the passageway. The inconsistencies before him were distressing. The corridor itself was both familiar and strange. He was certain he had been here before. There was that slender stone dripping cold water into the puddle below with melodious monotony, for instance. He had stood beside it many times, running his hands over its slick moistness and listening to the beauty of the drops.

Yet, even as he aimed his clicks *directly at it now, it changed like a living thing, growing until its tip actually touched the water, then shrinking back into the ceiling. Nearby, the mouth of a pit opened and closed menacingly. And the passage itself contracted and expanded as though it were a giant's lung.*

"Don't be afraid, Jared." *A gentle, feminine voice stirred the deep silence.* "It's just that we've forgotten how to keep things in place."

Her tone was soothing and familiar, yet unfamiliar and disturbing at the same time. He sent out precise clicks. *The impression returning from nearby was like a silhouette—as though he were hearing the woman only with back sounding. Her features were blank. And when he reached out, she wasn't there. Yet she spoke:*

"It's been so long, Jared! The details are all gone."

He went hesitantly forward. "Kind Survivoress?"

And he sensed her amusement. "You make it sound so stiff."

Instantly, an entire flight of misplaced childhood memories rushed back. "But you—weren't even real! You and Little Listener and the Forever Man—how can you be anything* but *a dream?"*

"Listen around you, Jared, Does any of this sound real?"

The hanging stone was still squirming. Rock brushed against his arm as the right wall closed in, then pulled away again.

Then he was only dreaming—just as he had dreamed, oh, so many times, so many gestations ago. He remembered with a pang of nostalgia how Kind Survivoress would take him by the hand and lead him off. It wasn't a hand he could always feel. And she didn't really take him anywhere, because he would be asleep on his ledge all the while.

Yet, suddenly he would be scampering in the familiar passage or in a nearby world with Little Listener, the boy who heard only the inaudible sounds of the minor insects. And Kind Survivoress would explain, "You and I, Jared, can keep the Listener from being lonesome. Just think how awful his world is—all pitch silent! But I can bring him into this passage, as I can bring you. When I do, it's as though he wasn't deaf anymore. And the two of you can play together."

Jared was fully back in the familiar-strange passageway now.

And Kind Survivoress offered, "Little Listener's a grown man. You wouldn't know him."

Confused, Jared said, "Dream things don't grow!"

"We're special dream things."

"Where's the Listener?" he asked skeptically. "Let me hear him."

"He and the Forever Man are fine. The Forever Man's old now, though. He's not really a Forever Man, you know—just almost. But there's no time to hear them. I'm worried about you, Jared. You've got to wake up!"

For a moment he almost felt as though he were going to break out of the dream. But then his thoughts went calmly back to his childhood. He remembered how Kind Survivoress had said he was the only one she could reach—and, even then, only when he was asleep. But he wouldn't stop telling people about her. And she was afraid because she knew others were beginning to wonder whether he might be a Different One. She didn't want the fate that befell all the Different Ones to befall him. So she had quit coming.

"You must wake up, Jared!" She interrupted his reminiscences. "You're hurt and you've been unconscious too long!"

"Is that all you came back for—just to wake me up?"

"No. I want to warn you about the monsters and about all the dreams I've heard you have—dreams of hunting for Light. The monsters are hideous and evil! I reached out and touched one's mind. It was so full of horrible, strange things that I couldn't stay in it for more than a fraction of a heartbeat!"

"There's more than one monster?"

"There are many of them."

"What about hunting Light?"

"Don't you hear, Jared, you're only chasing more dream stuff? There's no such thing as Darkness and Light, as you think of them. You're just trying to escape responsibility. There's Survivorship to think of, Unification—things that really mean something!"

He had always been sure that if his mother had lived she would have been quite like Kind Survivoress.

He started to answer her. But she was no longer there.

Jared rolled against the softness of a manna fiber mattress and felt the bandage on his head.

From somewhere in the distance, rising above the audible background, came a reassuring paternal voice pacing itself through the monotonous patter of the Familiarization Routine:

"... Here we are under the echo caster, son. Hear how loud it sounds? Notice the direction of the *clacks*—straight up. We're in the center of the world. Listen to how the echoes come back from all the walls at practically the same time. This way, boy ..."

Jared elevated himself on an unsteady elbow and someone caught his shoulders, easing him down again.

It was Adviser Lorenz, who turned his head the other way and urged, "Go tell the Wheel he's coming around."

Jared caught Della's receding scent as she left the recess. It had to struggle through the heavier odors clinging to everything around him—odors that identified Wheel Anselm's grotto.

From outside, the tutoring father's spiel bore back in on Jared's conscious, complicating his attempts to reorient himself.

"... There, directly before you, son—can you hear that empty space in the sound pattern? That's the entrance to our world. Now we're going over to the poultry yard. Watch it, boy! There's an outcropping about five paces in front of you. Let's stop here. Feel it. Get an idea of its size and shape. Try to hear it. Remember *exactly* where it is. And you'll save yourself many a bruised shin ... ."

Jared tried to banish the distracting voice and compose his thoughts. But the effects of his recent dream lay heavily upon him.

It was most odd that Kind Survivoress should emerge from his forgotten fantasies all of a sudden, as though he had reached back into the abyss of his past and brought forward a warm, memorable slice of childhood. But he recognized the manifestation for what it was—no more than a wistful yearning for the security he hadn't known since his own father had taken him by the hand and Familiarized him with his world, as that attentive father outside was doing now.

"What in Radiation happened?" he managed.

"You took a lance broadside on the temple," Lorenz reminded. "You've been out like an echo caster for a whole period."

Suddenly he remembered—everything. And he lurched up. "The monsters! The Zivvers!"

"They're gone—all of them."

"What happened?"

"Best we could make out was that the monster seized a Zivver at the entrance. Two other Zivvers tried to save him. But they just collapsed in their tracks."

Clacks from the central caster entered through parted curtains and bounced off the Adviser's face, carrying away a composite of his apprehensive expression. Something else was hidden among the wrinkles, adding further tautness to his closed eyelids—an uneasy hesitancy. The Adviser appeared to be deciding whether to say something.

Jared, however, was more concerned over the monster's having invaded the Upper Level. Until now, he had been certain the Barrier was adequate to keep the creature on the other side. He felt that he and Owen deserved whatever they had gotten for violating the taboos. But it didn't end there. Rather, the monster had crossed the Barrier to enter one of the worlds of man. And once more Jared wondered whether he might not be responsible. He had invaded the Original World first, hadn't he? And hadn't the monster picked a most convincing time to strike again—just when he was beginning to compound blasphemy by giving thought to resuming his search for Light?

The Adviser drew in a decisive breath. "What were you doing when you got hit by that spear?"

"Trying to reach the Zivver on guard at the entrance."

Lorenz stiffened audibly. "Then you *admit* it?"

"What's there to admit? I heard a chance to carry off a hostage."

"Oh." The word was shaded with disappointment. Then the Adviser added dubiously, "The Wheel will be glad to learn that. A lot of us wondered why you stole away."

Jared swung his legs over the side of the ledge. "I don't hear what you're trying to prove. You mean you think—"

But the other continued, "So you were going to *attack* a Zivver? That's a little hard to believe."

First there had been Lorenz's open hostility. Then there was his jestful—or perhaps only superficially jestful—suggestion that Jared's abilities were Zivverlike. Now this latest obscure insinuation. It all added up to *something*.

He caught the man's wrist. "What *do* you suspect?"

But just then Wheel Anselm swept the curtain aside and strode in. "What's all this about attacking a Zivver?"

Della followed him inside and Jared listened to her almost soundless motions as she came over to the slumber ledge.

"That's what he was trying to do when he made his way over to the entrance," Lorenz explained skeptically.

But Anselm missed the inflection. "Isn't that what I said he had in mind? How are you feeling, Jared my boy?"

"Like I was clouted with a lance."

The Wheel laughed patronizingly, then became serious. "You were closer to that thing than any of us. What in Radiation was it?"

Jared considered telling them about his previous experience with the monster. But the Law of the Barrier applied as rigidly here as in the Lower Level. "I don't know. I didn't have much time to listen to it before I took that lance."

"Cobalt," Adviser Lorenz murmured. "Must have been Cobalt."

47

"Might have been Cobalt *and* Strontium," Della suggested distantly. "Some got the impression there were *two* monsters."

Jared stiffened. Hadn't his dream, too, intimated there were more than one of the incredible creatures?

"Light—it was awful!" Anselm agreed. "It *must* have been the Twin Devils. What else could throw such uncanny things into your head like that?"

"It didn't, as you say, 'throw things' into everybody's head," the Adviser reminded officiously.

"True. Not all felt what I felt. For instance, none of the fuzzy-faces remember anything *that* odd."

"I don't either, and I'm not a fuzzy-face."

"There were a few *besides* the fuzzy-faces who didn't feel the sensations. How about you, my boy?"

"I don't know what you're talking about," Jared lied, sparing himself the necessity of going into details.

Anselm and Lorenz fell silent while Della laid a hand gently on Jared's forehead. "We're preparing something for you to eat. Is there anything else I can do?"

Confused, he trained an ear on the girl. She'd never spoken that charitably before!

"Well, my boy," Anselm said, backing off, "you take it easy for the rest of your stay—until you're ready to return home for With-drawal and Contemplation Against Unwise Unification."

The curtains swished as he and the Adviser left.

"I'll hear about that food," Della said, and followed them out.

Jared lay back on the ledge, exploring the soreness beneath the bandage. Still fresh in memory was his encounter with the monster—or monsters. In their presence, he had experienced the identical sensation he had felt in the Original World. For a mo-ment, as he recalled the impression of uncanny pressure on his face, it seemed as though his *eyes* had received most of the force. But why? And he was still puzzled that Owen hadn't experienced the peculiar feeling. Could his friend's closed-eyes preference possibly have had anything to do with his not having sensed the psychic pressure?

Della returned and he heard that she was carrying a shell filled with—he listened to the consistency of the liquid and sniffed its faint aroma—manna tuber broth. But he sensed more than that. There was something he couldn't identify in her other hand.

"Feel well enough for some of this?" She extended the bowl.

Her words had been feather-edged with concern and he was at a loss to explain her sudden change of heart.

Something warm dripped on his hand. "The broth," he cautioned, "you're spilling it."

"Oh." She leveled the bowl. "I'm sorry."

But he listened sharply at the girl. She hadn't even *heard* the liquid running down the outside of the shell. It was as though she were practically deaf!

Improvising a test, he whispered almost subvocally, "What kind of broth is this?"

There was no response. She had no fine hearing at all! Yet, after the formal dinner, she had heard well enough to use as a target the swirling fluidity of a pool so small and so silent that he hadn't even been aware of its presence.

She put the bowl on a nearby shelf and extended the object in her other hand. "What do you think of this, Jared?"

He inspected the thing. Clinging to it was the scent of the monster. It was tubular, like a manna stalk, but cut off on both ends. The smooth face of the larger end, however, was shattered. He ran a finger into the break and felt a hard, round object within. Withdrawing his finger, he cut it against something sharp.

"What is it?"

"I don't know. I found it at the entrance. I'm sure one of the monsters dropped it."

Again he felt the round thing behind the broken surface. It reminded him of—something.

"The big end was—warm when I picked it up," she disclosed.

He cast his ears warily on the girl. Why had she hesitated before the word "warm"? Did she know it was heat that Zivvers zivved? Was she furtively bringing up the subject so she could hear his reaction—perhaps even trying to test the Adviser's insinuation that he might be a Zivver? If that was her intention, it was well hidden.

Then he jolted erect. *Now* he remembered what the round object in the broken end of the tube reminded him of! It was a miniature version of the Holy Bulb used during religious services!

And he shook his head in bewilderment. What sense did *that* fool paradox make? Wasn't the Holy Bulb associated with Light—with goodness and virtue—rather than with hideous, evil monsters?

His remaining periods in the Upper Level were uneventful to the point of monotony. He found the people not at all friendly. Their experience with the monsters had left them apprehensive and distant. More than once his words had gone unheard while quickened heartbeats reflected lingering fear.

If it hadn't been for Della's presence, he might have returned home before his scheduled departure. As it was, though, the girl was a challenging enigma.

She stuck close by all the while. And the friendship she extended was so profuse that he often felt her hand slipping into his as she took him about the world acquainting him with the people.

On one occasion Della added to the mystery when she paused and whispered, "Jared, are you hiding something?"

"I don't know what you mean."

"I'm a pretty good marksman myself, don't you think?"

"With rocks—yes." He decided to nudge her on.

"And I'm the one who found that thing the monsters left behind."

"So?"

Her face was turned eagerly toward his and he studied her in the sound of the central caster. When he said nothing more, he heard her breathing become heavy with exasperation.

She turned to walk away but he caught her arm. "What do you *think* I'm hiding, Della?"

But her mood had changed. "Whether or not you've decided to Declare Unification Intentions."

That she was lying had been obvious.

Yet, throughout the final two periods she seemed to hang onto everything he said, as though his next words might be the very ones she wanted to hear. Even up to the moment of his departure her disposition was one of restrained expectancy.

They were standing by the manna orchard, with his escort party waiting at the entrance, when she said reproachfully:

"Jared, it isn't fair to hold anything back."

"Like what?"

"Like why you can—hear so well."

"The Prime Survivor spent all his time training me to—"

"You've told me all about that," she reminded impatiently. "Jared, if we're of the same mind after Withdrawal and Contemplation, we'll be Unified. It wouldn't be right to keep secrets then."

Just when he was at the point of demanding to know what she was driving at, Lorenz walked up with a bow slung over his shoulder.

"Before you leave," he said, "I thought you might give me a few pointers on archery."

Jared accepted the bow and quiver, wondering why Lorenz should suddenly want to improve his marksmanship. "Very well, I don't hear anybody over on the range."

"Oh, but the children will be playing there in a few beats," the Adviser dissented. "Listen at the orchard. Can you hear that tall manna plant right in front of you, about forty paces off?"

"I hear it."

"There's a fruit shell on the highest stalk. It ought to make a good enough target."

Backing well away from the vapors of the nearest boiling pit, Jared rattled a pair of clickstones. "With a stationary target," he explained, "you first have to sound it out clearly. The central caster doesn't give a precise impression."

He strung an arrow. "Then it's important not to move your feet, since you're oriented only in your original position."

Releasing the bowstring, he listened to the arrow pass more than two arm lengths above the shell.

Surprised that he should miss by that much, he sounded the stones again. But from the corner of his hearing he caught

Lorenz's reaction. The Adviser's expression was one of nearly irrepressible excitement. Della, too, wore an almost ecstatic tone on her face.

Why should they be overjoyed because he had failed to hit the shell? Bewildered, he strung another arrow and let it fly.

It went astray by the same distance.

Now the Adviser and the girl sounded even more jubilant. But Lorenz exuded triumph, whereas Della seemed intensely gratified.

He missed with two more shots before he wearied of their incomprehensible game. Annoyed, he dropped the bow and quiver and headed for the exit where the escort party awaited. After he had gone several paces he realized why his aim had been off. Standard bowstring tension here was greater than in his world! It was that simple. He even remembered now that the string had felt stiffer.

Then he stopped short. Abruptly he heard everything clearly. He *knew* why Lorenz had reacted as he had when the arrows missed—even why the archery exhibition had been arranged in the first place.

In order to protect his status as Adviser, Lorenz was intent on disqualifying him from Unification with Della. What better way than to prove him a Zivver?

The Adviser must have known Zivvers couldn't ziv in the heat of an orchard-hot springs area. And, since Jared had consistently missed the target there, Lorenz must now be *certain* he was a Zivver.

But what was the girl's interest? Evidently she also knew of the Zivvers' limitation. And she had recognized what the test might prove, even though she may not have known it was contrived specifically for that purpose.

But, then, she had actually been *elated* over his failure to hit the shell. Why?

"Jared! Jared!"

He listened to Della running forward to overtake him.

She caught his arm. "You don't have to tell me now. I know. Oh, Jared, Jared! I never dreamed anything like this would happen!"

She drew his head down and kissed him.

"You know—what?" he asked, drawing her out.

She went on effusively, "Don't you hear I suspected it all along—from the moment you threw the spears? And when I brought you that tube the monster dropped I all but said I had found it by its *heat*. I couldn't make the first move, though—not until I was certain you were a Zivver too."

From the depths of his astonishment, he managed to ask, "*Too?*"

"Yes, Jared. I'm a Zivver—just like you."

The Captain of the Official Escort came over from the entrance. "We're ready whenever you are."

CHAPTER FIVE

RIGID SELF-DISCIPLINE WAS CUSTOMARY IN Withdrawal and Contemplation. So crucial a decision called for searching introspection. For Unification automatically meant full Survivorship—a double measure of responsibility. Then too, one so dedicated also had to concern himself with the demanding obligations of Procreating and Familiarization of Progeny.

These considerations were far from Jared's mind over the next few periods, however, as he meditated in the silence of his heavily curtained grotto. He thought of Della—yes. But certainly not in the sound of normal Unification. Rather, his speculation centered on the significance of her being a Zivver. How had she managed to conceal that fact? And what were her intentions?

At that, though, the situation was not without humor. There was Lorenz—on a Zivver hunt. And all the while he had one right beside his ear! As far as Jared was concerned, the girl would be conveniently available for counteraccusation should the Adviser ever decide to accuse *him* of being a Zivver.

If he so chose, he could expose her any time he wanted. But what would he gain? Anyway, the fact that *she* thought *he* was a Zivver made for an interesting situation and he was anxious to hear what would come of it.

This line of thought invariably led to conjecture on the nature of zivving. What magical power was it that permitted one to know where things were in total silence and in the absence of odors? Or, like his imaginary Little Listener, did Zivvers hear

54

some sort of soundless noise made by all things, animate and inanimate alike? Then he remembered it wasn't sound at all, but heat that they zivved.

Each time his attention wandered to these irrelevant matters, he knew he was not rendering full service to the spirit of Withdrawal and Contemplation. Yet, he supposed all of these subjects deserved exploration under the special conditions of his Unification.

He spared himself one possible distraction, though, in not telling the Prime Survivor about the monsters' invasion of the Upper Level. That would only have revived condemnation of his trip to the Original World.

On the fourth period of retreat he was jolted from meditation by a commotion in the world outside. At first he thought the monsters had reached the Lower Level. But there was not so much consternation as dismay in the voices of those streaming toward the orchard.

They had all abandoned the residential area by the time he decided on interrupting Withdrawal. He started after them. But halfway across the world, the central caster fetched impressions of the Prime Survivor and Elder Haverty coming in his direction.

"How long did you *expect* to keep it a secret?" Haverty was asking.

"Until I could decide what to do about it, at least," the Prime Survivor answered glumly.

"Eh? What? I mean, what *can* you do about something like that?"

But the other had detected Jared. "So you broke Withdrawal," he observed. "I suppose it's just as well."

Haverty excused himself, explaining that he was going to hear if Elder Maxwell had any ideas on how to cope with the situation.

"What happened?" Jared asked after the other had gone.

"We've just had nine hot springs go dry." The Prime Survivor led the way toward their grotto.

Jared was relieved. "Oh, I thought it might be soubats, or maybe Zivvers."

"I wish to Light that's *all* it was."

In the curtain-shielded privacy of their recess, the Prime Survivor paced aimlessly. "This is a critical situation, Jared!"

"Maybe the springs will start flowing again."

"The other three that dried up haven't started again. I'm afraid they're out for good."

Jared shrugged. "So we'll have to do without them."

"Don't you hear the seriousness of this thing? We have a tight, delicate balance here. What's happened might well mean some of us *won't be able to survive!*"

Jared started to offer further encouragement. But suddenly he was preoccupied with self-concern. Was this part of the pattern of punishment he had brought on by provoking the Original World monster? Hot springs going dry in both the Upper and Lower Level, evil beings pushing past the Barrier—were they all actually strokes of vengeance by an offended Light Almighty?

"What do you mean—'some of us won't be able to survive'?"

"Figure it out yourself. Each hot spring feeds the tendrils of a hundred and twenty-five manna plants at the most. Nine dead boiling pits means almost twelve hundred fewer plants."

"But that's just a fraction—"

"Any fraction that reduces the survival potential is a critical factor. If we apply the formula, we hear that with nine less hot springs we can support only thirty-four head of cattle instead of forty. All the other livestock will have to be reduced proportionately. In the long run it will mean seventeen less people can exist here!"

"Well make up the difference with more game."

"There'll be *less* game—with more soubats than ever flying the passageways."

The Prime Survivor stopped pacing and stood there breathing heavily. Clickstone echoes weren't needed to tell that he was crestfallen, that the creases in his face were etched even more deeply.

Jared couldn't escape a sense of helplessness as he thought of man's absolute dependence on the manna plants. Actually, they stood between the Survivors and death, providing as they did food for humans and livestock alike; rich juices; fibers for the women to twist into cloths, ropes, and fishing nets; shells that could be split in half and used as containers; stalks that could be dried out sufficiently for sharpening into a spear or arrow.

Now, almost bitterly, he could recall his father's voice finding new depths of respect and thoughtfulness gestations ago in reciting one of the legends:

"Our manna trees are a copy of the magnificent plants created by Light in Paradise—but a poor copy indeed. Light's creation was topped by thousands of gracious, lacy things that swayed in the breeze and made whispering noises while they enjoyed constant communion with the Almighty. They drank of His energy and used it in such a manner as to mix the water they drank with bits of soil and with the air that men and animals breathed out. And they transformed these things into food and pure air for man and animal alike.

"But Light's plant wasn't *good enough*. It seems we had to fashion a tree without the graceful, whispering things at the top—one which has, instead, great masses of awkward feelers that grow deep into the boiling pits. There they draw energy from the water's heat and use it to transform the foul air of the worlds and passageways and the elements from compost into fibers and tubers, fruit and fresh air."

That was the manna plant.

"What are we going to do about the hot-springs situation?" Jared asked finally.

"How are you coming along with Contemplation?"

"I suppose I've just about exhausted the subject."

"That helps." The Prime Survivor lodged a hand on his shoulder. "I've an idea there's going to be drastic need for help from the Upper Level before long. You realize, of course, that you don't have much of a choice in Contemplation. Under the circumstances, this Unification couldn't *possibly* be Unwise."

"No. I don't suppose it could."

The Prime Survivor cuffed his arm warmly. "I'm sure you'll be ready to return to the Upper Level just as soon as the Seven Periods of Withdrawal are over."

Outside, a deep silence that had fallen over the world was interrupted by the first phrases of the Litany of Light. The Guardian of the Way's fervent voice cracked with veneration as he shouted out the Recitations. More subdued but no less reverent were the Responses by the worshippers.

Recalling that Revitalization Ceremonies had failed after the first three springs had gone dry, Jared brushed the curtain aside and headed for the Assembly Area to join the services. That it would be a novel experience added little to his enthusiasm.

He stayed on the fringe of the Congregation. To have gone up front at the first ceremony he had attended in gestations would have distracted Guardian and Survivors alike. And he felt even more self-conscious when he heard a sharp-eared child nearby grip his mother's arm and exclaim, "It's Jared, Mother! It's Jared Fenton!"

"Hush and listen to the Guardian!" the woman reproved.

Guardian Philar was circulating among them, his words rebounding clearly from the object he clutched against his chest.

"Feel this Holy Bulb," he exhorted. "Be inspired along the passageway of virtue. Let us hurl back Darkness. Only by renouncing evil can we discharge our obligations as Survivors and listen ahead to that great period when we will be Reunited with Light Almighty!"

If the Guardian of the Way wasn't the gauntest man in the Lower Level, Jared felt certain, then he was at least in close running for the distinction. Bouncing off his body, central caster echoes picked up the harsh bluntness of bones that threatened to erupt through skin. His beard was sparse to the extreme of being fully inaudible. But the most prominent features of his haggard face were eyes set deep in their sockets and lids squeezed so firmly together that it was doubtful whether they had ever been open.

He reached Jared and paused, his voice stooping for but not quite finding a bass fervor. "Among all the things in this world, our Holy Bulb is the only one that has ever been in contact with Light. Feel it." And, when Jared hesitated, *"Feel it!"*

His hand went out reluctantly and touched its cold, round surface. In exaggerated proportion, it had the same properties as the miniature Bulb in the object the monsters had left in the Upper Level. And he wondered ...

But he banished the thought. Wasn't it his own curiosity—over the Bulb and many other things—that had gotten the worlds into their present predicament?

The Guardian moved on, swaying, almost chanting. "There are those who would deny that Light ever dwelt in this relic. To them goes the blame for having provoked the Almighty's wrath."

Jared lowered his head, aware that many around him would have no trouble identifying the person for whom the accusation was intended.

"So the spiritual challenge we face on this Revitalization Period," the Guardian concluded, "is a personal one. The echoes from the wall are clear. Unless we atone individually for our misdeeds, we may expect to find that the same Light Almighty who banished Survivor from His presence has it in His power to destroy Survivor completely!"

He replaced the Holy Bulb in its niche and faced the Congregation, arms outstretched. An elderly woman went and stood humbly before him and Jared listened to Philar's hands performing the final ritual.

"Do you feel Him?" the Guardian demanded.

The woman grunted a disappointed negative reply and moved on.

"Patience, daughter. Effective Excitation comes to all those who persevere against Darkness."

Another Survivoress, two children and a Survivor humbled themselves in front of Guardian Philar before the first positive response was evoked in the Excitation of the Optic Nerve Ceremony. It was elicited from a young woman. As soon as the Guardian brushed aside the veil of hair that hung in front of her face and applied fingertips to her eyelids she cried out ecstatically:

"I feel Him! Oh, I feel Him!"

The stark emotion in the woman's voice made Jared's flesh tingle.

Patting her head approvingly, the Guardian turned to the next person.

Jared lagged behind the last in line, not letting himself imagine those who were Effectively Excited might actually be feeling nothing more than a special pressure from the Guardian's hands. Rather, he tried to keep his thoughts receptive, so that his first participation in the ritual would not be thwarted by long-standing prejudice.

By the time his turn arrived, the others had gone from the Assembly Area leaving only him and the Guardian. Waiting with his head lowered, he listened to Philar's severe expression. The Guardian was not concealing his belief that Jared's flagrant disrespect for the Barrier had brought on the Lower Level's misfortunes.

Bony hands reached out to Jared's face. They explored their way along his cheeks to his eyes. Then fingernails pressed into the soft recesses beneath the lower lids.

At first there was—nothing. Then the Guardian applied an almost painful pressure.

"Do you feel Him!" he demanded.

But Jared only stood there confounded. *Two fuzzy half rings of silent sound were dancing around in his head.* He could feel them *not* where the Guardian was pressing, but somewhere near the upper area of his eyeballs. Effective Excitation was the same sort of sensation he had twice experienced in the presence of the monsters!

Was he actually supposed to be feeling a part of Light Himself? If so, then why should he be aware of the presence of the Almighty, in a slightly different way, whenever he was near the Twin Devils? If Light was good, then why should He also be associated with the evil creatures?

Jared repressed the profane thoughts, chasing them completely out of his mind, together with the memory of ever having entertained them.

Fascinated, he listened to the dancing rings. They became more or less vivid as the Guardian varied the pressure of his fingernails.

"Are you feeling Him?"

"I feel Him," Jared admitted weakly.

"I didn't expect you would," the other said, somewhat disappointed. "But I'm glad to hear there's still hope for you."

He went over and sat on a ledge below the Holy Bulb niche and his voice lost some of its sharpness. "We haven't heard too much of you over here, Jared. Your father's been concerned about that and I can understand why. Some period the destiny of this world will be in your hands. Will they be *good* hands?"

Jared lowered himself on the ledge and sat there with his head bowed. "I *felt* Him," he mumbled. "I *felt* Him."

"Of course you did, son." The Guardian laid a sympathetic hand on his arm. "You could have felt Him sooner than this, you know. And things would have been different for you—different, perhaps, for the whole world."

"Did *I* cause the hot springs to dry up?"

"I can think of nothing that would enrage the Almighty more than violation of the Barrier taboo."

Jared's hands clutched each other in distress. "What can I do?"

"You can atone. Then we'll hear what happens afterward."

"But you don't understand. It may be more than just violating the Barrier! I've thought Light might not be Almighty, that He—"

"I do understand, son. You've had your doubts, like other Survivors from time to time. But remember—in the long run, one isn't to be judged by his skepticism. The true measure of a reconverted Survivor is the sincerity with which he renounces his disbeliefs."

"Do you think I can find the right amount of sincerity?"

"I'm sure you can—now that we've had this talk. And I've no doubt that should promised Reunion with Light come during your time, you'll be prepared for it."

The Guardian trained his ears on infinity. "What a beautiful period that will be, Jared—Light all around us, touching everything, a Constant Communion, with the Almighty bringing man total knowledge of all things about him. And Darkness will be erased completely."

Jared spent the rest of that period in the seclusion of his grotto. Unification, however, was not the subject of his Contemplation.

Instead, he reviewed his new persuasions, careful not to entertain any thoughts that might be offensive to the Almighty.

In that single quarter period he renounced his dedicated search for Darkness and Light, denying himself any regret over having done so. And he resolved he would never again go beyond the Barrier.

New convictions firmly implanted, he relaxed in the assurance that everything would be all right—spiritually and physically. So certain did it seem he had done the proper thing that he wouldn't have been at all surprised to hear the twelve dry springs had begun running again. It was as though he had entered into a covenant with Light.

He was still reaffirming his resolution when the Prime Survivor entered. "The Guardian just told me you'd heard the sound, son."

"I hear a lot of things I didn't hear before." The earnest words bathed his father's face and carried back with them the outline of a smile that was warm with approval and pride.

"I've been waiting for you to speak like this for a long time, Jared. It means I can now go ahead with my plans."

"What plans?"

"This world should have young, vital leadership. It lacked that even *before* the springs went dry. With this challenge facing us, we need the imagination of a youthful leader all the more."

"You want me to become Prime Survivor?"

"As soon as possible. It'll take plenty of preparation. But I'll give you all the help I can."

A half-dozen periods earlier, Jared would have had no part of this development. But now it seemed only a minor enlargement of the life of dedicated purpose to which he had pledged himself.

"I don't hear any arguments," the Prime Survivor said gratefully.

"You won't. Not if this is the way you want it."

"Good! Over the next couple of periods I'll tell you some of the things that have to be done. Then, when you get back from the Upper Level, we'll start our formal training."

"How are the Elders going to take this?"

"After they heard what went on between you and Guardian Philar, they didn't have any objections at all."

Early the next period—even before the central echo caster had been turned on—Jared was shaken roughly from his sleep.

"Wake up! Something's happened!"

It was Elder Averyman. And whatever had happened must have been serious, indeed, for him to have burst into a private grotto.

Jared bounded to his feet, conscious of his brother's restless stirring on the next ledge. "What is it?" he demanded.

"The Prime Survivor!" Averyman broke for the exit. "Come—quick!"

Jared raced off after him, hearing both that Romel was awakening and that his father's ledge was empty. He overtook the Elder near the entrance to the world. "Where are we going?"

But Averyman only huffed more erratically. And the rush of air into and out of his lungs was chopped into discontinuous sound by the motion of the hair that hung down over his face.

That something was seriously amiss was evidenced by more than the Elder's behavior. Indistinct voices, muffled in apprehension, could be heard in small, scattered groups. And Jared listened to several other persons, who had evidently been up and about soon enough to hear what had happened, racing toward the entrance.

"It's the Prime Survivor!" Averyman managed between gasps. "We were out for our early walk. And he was saying how he was going to let you take over. When we passed by the entrance—" He stumbled and Jared crashed into his flailing form.

Someone turned on the central caster and Jared oriented himself as the details of his world sprang into audibility all around him. Among the impressions came that of Romel plodding along after them.

Elder Averyman brought his breathing under control. "It was awful! This thing came rushing from the passage, all fluttering and foul smelling! Your father and I could only stand there terrified—"

The smell of the monster still clung to the air. Detecting it, Jared raced ahead.

"Then there was this hissing sound," Averyman's laboring voice receded. "And the Prime Survivor fell where he stood. He didn't move—not even when the thing came for him!"

Jared reached the entrance and elbowed his way past several Survivors who were asking one another what had happened.

The odor was even more offensive in the Passageway, growing stronger in the direction of the Original World. Mingled with it was the familiar scent of the Prime Survivor. There seemed to be an accumulation of the stench a short distance away. Jared followed his nose to the spot, reaching down to pick up something soft and limp.

About twice the size of his hand, it felt like manna cloth. Only, the texture was incomparably finer. And from each corner dangled a ribbon of the same material.

It was something that certainly required further study. But, as long as it reeked with the smell of the monster, he couldn't bring it into the world without causing commotion. So he put it down and scraped dirt over it, fixing the location of the spot in his mind.

On the way back he almost collided with his brother, who was groping along the passageway.

"It sounds like you'll be Prime Survivor sooner than you expected," Romel said, not without a trace of envy in his voice.

CHAPTER SIX

"... WE THEREFORE HUMBLY INVOKE the guidance of Light Almighty as we rededicate ourselves under new leadership."

Survivor Averyman, as Senior Elder, was bringing his speech to a close. He paused and listened out over the Assembly.

Standing behind him, Jared too heard the silence, relieved only by the soft flow of many tense breaths. It was an anxious stillness, rather than one that bore respect for the Investiture Ceremonies.

Nor could he himself muster much attention for the Elder's words. His thoughts were overburdened with bitterness. It wasn't as much that Light had broken the covenant as it was that He had decided on so ruthless a means of making that fact clear.

That the Prime Survivor was gone forever from the worlds of man was, for Jared, a tragedy. On several occasions over the past two periods he would have gone charging defiantly up the passageway had it not been for the remote possibility that the loss of his father was only temporary, to test the sincerity of his repentance. A more practical reason he hadn't tried to track down the monster was that Protectors had been stationed at the entrance.

He sneezed and sniffled, evoking a disdainful pause in Survivor Averyman's speech. After a moment, the Elder resumed:

"We must not expect from our new Prime Survivor the forehearing and wisdom that we came to associate with his late father. For what *could* compare with an understanding deep enough to hear ahead to the imminent necessity of preparing his successor?"

65

Jared listened impatiently over toward the guarded entrance. There was yet another reason he couldn't go plunging beyond the Barrier in search of his father. That would only call the wrath of the Elders down on his head and they would make Romel the Prime Survivor—a development which could bring only chaos to the world.

Someone nudged him forward and he found himself standing in front of the Guardian of the Way.

"Repeat after me," Philar said solemnly, "'I swear that I will bend all effort to the Challenge of Survival, not only for myself but in behalf of every individual in the Lower Level.'"

Struggling through the vow, Jared interrupted his flow of words with a sniffle.

"'I dedicate myself,'" the Guardian went on, "'to the needs of all who depend upon me and I will do whatever I can to draw aside the Curtain of Darkness—so help me Light!'"

Jared punctuated the final word with a sneeze.

Investiture over, he remained in front of the Official Grotto receiving perfunctory handshakes.

Romel was the last to approach. "Now the fun begins," he said facetiously. The words were not as relaxed as they might have been, though, and they offered no clue as to what expression was silenced by the obscuring veil of hair.

"I'll need a lot of help," Jared admitted. "It won't be easy."

"I didn't think it would." Romel wasn't successfully concealing his envy. "Of course, the first thing will be to finish the hearing."

Interrupted by Investiture, the hearing wasn't Jared's concern, however. It was being conducted by the Elders, who were even now filing back into the Official Grotto. And there was no doubt that its mention had been subtly intended to lead to something else. For a moment Jared could almost hear the familiar *hiss* of the swish-rope.

"Do you suppose," Romel continued, unnecessarily loud, "that the monster that got the Prime Survivor was anything like the one you heard in the Original World?"

There it was—the tightening of the coils around his ankles. Romel wasn't going to let anyone forget Jared had violated the

Barrier taboo. Slack was being taken on the rope. The violent tug would come later.

"I wouldn't know," he rapped out, following the last of the witnesses into the Official Grotto.

A portable caster had been set in operation and Jared, taking his place at the meeting slab, concentrated on its *clicks* as modified by the persons in the recess. All the Elders were in their places while the witnesses were grouped off to one side.

"I believe we were listening to Survivor Metcalf," Elder Averyman said. "He was telling us what he heard."

A lean, nervous man came forward and stood beside the slab. Quite audibly, his fingers enmeshed, squirmed against one another, freed themselves and locked again.

"I couldn't catch its sound too clearly," he apologized. "I was just coming from the orchard when I heard you and the Prime Survivor shouting. I picked my impression of the thing off the echoes from your voices."

"And what did it sound like?"

"I don't know. Something about the size of a man, I suppose."

It was disconcerting the way the witness kept moving his head from side to side. He was a fuzzy-face and the rippling motion of the hair streaming down in front reminded Jared of the fluttering flesh of the Original World monster.

"Did you hear its face?" Averyman asked.

"No. I was too far away."

"What about an—uncanny sound?"

"I don't recall anything like a *silent* sound, like some of the others heard."

Metcalf was a fuzzy-face. So was Averyman, as were two others who had testified. And not one of those four had gotten psychic impressions of a roaring silence, Jared remembered. Even in the Upper Level none of the fuzzy-faces had heard the incredible, inaudible noise made by the monsters.

Jared cleared his throat, and swallowed painfully, coughed several times and gripped his neck. He'd never felt like *this* before.

Averyman dismissed the witness and called another.

By now, the two periods of hearings had become tedious. After all, there were really only two categories of witnesses—those who had heard the supernatural sound and those who hadn't.

More important, as far as Jared was concerned, was the personal matter of his growing uncertainty. He wasn't so sure now that the monsters were a punishment for his defiance of the Barrier. That the horrible menace had *not* ended with his sincere atonement could mean only one of two things: Light would accept *no* degree of repentance, or his visit to the Original World had not, after all, aggravated the monsters.

Then he drew attentively erect as a third possibility suggested itself: Suppose he was right about Light and Darkness being *physical* things. Suppose, in his search for the two, he had almost uncovered a significant truth. And suppose the monsters, assuming that they were opposed to his success, were aware of how close he had come. Wouldn't they do everything possible to discourage him?

A violent sneeze snapped his head back and elicited a reproving silence from Averyman, who had been in the middle of a question.

The new witness was a young boy whose excited account left no doubt that *he* had heard the impossible sounds.

"And how would you describe these—sensations?" Elder Averyman completed the question.

"It was like a lot of crazy shouts that kept bouncing against my face. And when I put my hands over my ears I kept on hearing them."

The child's head had been turned toward Averyman and Jared couldn't hear the details of his face. But suddenly it seemed vitally important that he should know the boy's characteristic expression. So he went around the slab, seized his shoulders and held him with his features fully exposed to the portable caster.

It was as he had expected—the child's eyes were wide open.

"You have something you'd like to say?" Averyman asked, not quite concealing his resentment over the interruption.

"No—nothing." Jared returned to his place.

The boy was an open-eyed type. Jared, himself, was open-eyed. Three other witnesses had fallen into the same category. And *all* of them had felt the strange sensations!

Was it as he had guessed once before—that the silent sound might in some way be connected with the eyes, provided they were exposed? And now he recalled how strangely his own eyes had reacted during the Excitation of the Optic Nerve Ceremony. The weird rings of noise had clearly seemed to be dancing beneath his lids, hadn't they?

But what significance could be drawn from all this? If the eyes were intended only for feeling Light, then why was it they could also sense the evil of the monsters? He was both excited and confused by the flood of inspirational questions. And he was annoyed that the same inspiration would produce none of the answers.

Since the eyes seemed to be the common element between Divinity and Devil, he asked himself queasily, could Light be in some sort of evil conspiracy with the monsters?

There! He had entertained the sacrilegious thought! And he braced himself for the wrath of the Almighty.

But, instead, there came only a direct question from Elder Averyman: "Well, Jared—rather, Your Survivorship—you've heard these various descriptions. How do they compare with your impressions of that monster in the Original World?"

He decided to play it a bit shrewder. "I'm not so sure I heard a monster. You know how your imagination can run away with you." There was no sense in calling attention to his experience with the creature. Nor did he hear where he could gain anything by telling them about the beings that had invaded the Upper Level.

"Eh? What?" Elder Haverty inquired. "You mean you *didn't* hear a monster in the Original World? You *did* go there, didn't you?"

Jared tried to clear his throat, but the painful roughness persisted. "Yes, I went there."

"And a lot has happened since then," Survivor Maxwell reminded. "We've lost some hot springs. A monster has carried off the Prime Survivor. Do you suppose you're to blame for those misfortunes?"

"No, I don't think so." Why incriminate himself?

"Some think you might be," Averyman said stiffly.

Jared sprang up. "If this is an attempt to remove me from—"

"Sit down, son," Maxwell urged. "Elder Averyman said we had to make you Prime Survivor. But there's nothing to keep us from easing you out if we think that's best."

"The question," Haverty repeated, "is whether you're the cause of all that's happened to this world."

"Of course I'm not! Those first three hot springs went dry long before I crossed the Barrier!"

There was a speculative silence around the slab. But Jared was more surprised than any of them by the truth he had spontaneously spoken. It had opened his ears to a whole flood of realization.

"Don't you understand?" He leaned tensely over the slab, letting sound from the portable caster play over his face so the others could hear his sincerity. "What's happening now *couldn't* be because I went across the Barrier! The Upper Level's having the *same troubles!* They lost some boiling pits and one of their Survivors turned up missing *before I even went to the Original World!*"

"We'd be more likely to believe that," Averyman pointed out cynically, "if you'd told us about it earlier."

"I didn't realize I had crossed the Barrier *after* those things had happened. And I figured that if I told you about them you'd only be more certain I was to blame."

"Eh?" Haverty put in. "How do we know you're telling the truth about the Upper Level having trouble too?"

"Get the Official Escort to ask about it when they take me back up there."

Jared felt like a Survivor who had been freed from the depths of Radiation. He had cast off shackles of superstition that would have thrown a curtain of fear over the rest of his life.

His relief was almost boundless—knowing that his trip to the Original World to hunt for Darkness and Light had not provoked the vengeance of an aggrieved Almighty Power. It meant there was no dire necessity of relinquishing that search. Of course, he wouldn't be able to devote as much effort to the quest as he had planned—not with his Prime Survivorship a reality and with Unification hanging over his head. But, at least, he could go on with it.

A depression that he had known for many periods melted away before his exuberance. He would have felt like shouting had it not been for the fact that his throat was bothering him again.

He sneezed and his head started throbbing.

A few moments later Elder Maxwell sneezed too, then sniffled.

Abruptly there was a disturbance in the world outside and Jared tensed as he caught a whiff of the monster's stench.

Someone swept into the grotto and quickly placated, "Don't be alarmed by the smell." The voice was Romel's. "It's coming from something in my hand—something the monster dropped when it carried off the Prime Survivor."

Jared intercepted the *clicks* from the portable caster as they echoed against the object his brother was displaying. It was the cloth he had buried in the passageway. Romel was firming his grip on that imaginary swish-rope. And Jared waited for the tug that would jerk him off his feet.

The elders had had time to study the reeking object, and Maxwell asked, "Where did you get this thing?"

"I listened to Jared hide it. And I dug it up."

"Why would he do a thing like that?"

"Ask *him*." But before Maxwell could, Romel went on, "I think he was covering up for the monster. Don't get me wrong now. Jared's my brother. But the interest of the Lower Level comes first. That's why I'm exposing this conspiracy."

"That's ridiculous—" Jared began.

"Eh? What?" Haverty interrupted. "Conspiracy? What conspiracy? Why should your brother conspire with the monster? How *could* he conspire with it?"

"He stole off and met it in the Original World, didn't he?"

Echoes fetched only the impression of hair hanging down over Romel's face. But Jared knew that the smile concealed beneath the veil was as sardonic as it had been each time the swish-rope accomplished its mischievous purpose during an earlier era.

"I hid the cloth," he began, "because—"

But Haverty persisted. "What would he gain by conspiring with a monster?"

There was yet another tug to be had from the swish-rope. "He's Prime Survivor now, isn't he?" Romel reminded with a laugh.

Jared lunged up. But two Elders halted his charge.

"That kind of outburst," Averyman assured, "only makes the accusation seem more reasonable."

Jared relaxed before the slab. "I hid the cloth because I wanted to study it later. I couldn't very well bring it into the world without having to answer the same questions I'm answering now."

"Reasonable," Averyman grumbled. "And what about this matter of conspiring with the monster?"

"Would you say I'd have anything to gain if a monster kidnapped a Zivver?"

"Not personally, no."

He told them about the invasion of the Upper Level by the two monsters.

"And why didn't you say anything about this before?" Averyman asked somewhat indignantly after he had finished.

"For the same reason I've already given—I didn't realize then that I *wasn't* responsible for what was happening."

After a moment Maxwell warned, "We certainly intend to check that story about the Zivver being carried off by monsters."

"If you find out I'm lying, give me any length of sentence in the Punishment Pit."

Averyman rose. "I think this hearing has taken up enough time for one period."

"Hearing? Compost!" Jared swore. "Let's quit sitting on our hands and go after the Prime Survivor!"

"Easy now," Haverty soothed. "We don't want to do anything rash. We may be dealing with Cobalt and Strontium themselves."

"But they'll be back!"

"At which time we'll rely both on the Protectors we've posted at the entrance and on the Guardian for Exorcism."

It was a stupid position born of deaf superstition. But Jared heard that he wouldn't be able to budge them from it.

Later that period he withdrew to the Fenton Grotto to work on a formula for reallocating the remaining manna husk output among Survivors and livestock. Hunched over the sandbox, he brushed the writing area smooth and began all over again with his stylus. But a violent sneeze swept the surface clean and he threw the instrument down in disgust.

He pushed the box aside and laid his head on the slab. Not only were the sniffles driving him out of his mind, but he also felt as though his head were stuffed with warm, moist wool. He'd had fever before, but not like this. Nor had he ever heard of anyone else being sick in this manner.

Leading his thoughts away from physical discomfort, he took cheer from the still unbelievable realization that no Divine Being stood in the way of his quest for Light. The monsters might resent his seeking Darkness and Light. But they could be resisted—if he could only find some way to get around their sleep-dealing powers.

It was tantalizing, too, how everything seemed to point toward some vast and incomprehensible pattern into which were woven so many material and immaterial things. What was the obscure relationship between the eyes and Light, Light and Darkness, Darkness and the Original World, the Original World and Radiation? The apparent linkage extended to the Twin Devils then, in a great circle, back again to the eyes and the Light-Darkness arrangement.

He found himself recalling Cyrus, the Thinker, who spent his time meditating in his grotto at the other end of the world. He remembered that gestations ago he had heard the old man express some novel ideas on Darkness. Perhaps it was those philosophic sessions that had suggested the search for Darkness—*and* Light—in the first place. And Jared knew he must talk with the Thinker again—soon.

The curtains parted, admitting Many, one of the new Survivors.

"For a P.S. of only a few heartbeats' experience," he chided, "you've sure carved out a chunk of trouble for yourself—popping off before the Elders about chasing after the monster."

Jared laughed. "Guess I should have kept my mouth shut."

Many perched on the slab beside him and sneezed. "The Guardian hit the dome when he heard about it. He says now he's sure Romel would make a better P.S."

"After I hear my way clear with this hot-springs emergency, I'll straighten him out."

"He's saying the way you acted at the hearing proves you haven't atoned. And he's predicting more misfortune for the world."

As though Many's words had also been a cue for fulfillment of Guardian Philar's prophesy, distressed voices began filtering through the curtain.

Plunging outside, Jared snagged one of the men who were racing by. "What's all the commotion?"

"The river! It's running dry!"

Even before he reached the bank, the central caster's *clacks* fetched a composite of the situation. The river had fallen so alarmingly below its normal level that the liquid softness of its reflected sound was completely hidden in the echo void of the bank. And there came only the enfeebled gurgling of water around rocks that had never before been exposed.

A terrified scream shrilled from the direction of the main entrance and, without breaking stride, Jared altered course.

With the central caster behind him, he began getting a better impression of what lay ahead. The Protectors stationed at the mouth of the passageway were in a state of agitated disorder.

"Monster! Monster!" someone over there was shouting.

Then Jared checked his charge as the entire tunnel abruptly began roaring with the soundless noise of the monsters. The sensations he received were like Effective Excitation amplified a thousandfold. But now there were no fuzzy half rings of inaudible sound touching his eyeballs, as in the Optic Nerve Ceremony. Instead, the screaming silence was like a detached, impersonal thing—something associated not with any part of himself, but rather with the mouth of the tunnel!

It was more than that, however. The noiselessness leaked off, much like valid sound, and touched many things—the dome, the wall on his right, the hanging stones beside the entrance.

Starting forward again, he threw his hands in front of his face. The distant, whispering roar of Effective Excitation left him immediately. Then that *proved* it—the uncanny stuff that came from monsters *did* inflict its weird pressure *on his eyes!*

Spared the confusing sensations, he concentrated now on the echoes coming from ahead. There was no monster in the entrance. That one had been there only a few beats earlier was borne out by the loitering scent. And his ears picked out the tubular object that lay on the floor of the tunnel. Even from this distance he could hear it was like the one Della had found in the Upper Level.

Just as he reached the entrance, one of the Protectors raised a rock over his head and raced toward the tube.

"No! Don't!" Jared shouted.

The guard hurled the rock.

Eyes exposed again, Jared reached down for the remains of the object. It was warm and it rattled and tinkled when he shook it.

He noticed, too, that there were no more traces of the screaming silence.

CHAPTER SEVEN

LIVING ALONE AND SERVED HIS necessities by the widowed women of the Lower Level, Cyrus spent his time immersed in himself. When the opportunity to speak materialized, however, his tongue diligently set about the task of making up for long stretches of idleness.

Now, for instance, the Thinker was holding forth on many subjects, seemingly all at the same time:

"Jared Fenton. *Prime Survivor* Jared Fenton, mind you! Back for another session—just like we used to have gestations ago."

Jared shifted impatiently on the bench beside him. "I wanted to ask about—"

"But I'm afraid you've got your work cut out for you—what with the hot springs trickling out and those monsters running around the passages. Have you decided what's to be done about the river going dry? And that thing the monster left behind yesterperiod—what do you suppose it was?"

"It seems to me that—"

"Hold it! I'd like to think this thing out a bit."

Jared was more than grateful for the few moments' silence. It brought relief to his pounding head, which threatened to split like a manna shell each time he coughed. He'd had fever before—when he was bitten by a spider, for instance. But it was never like this.

Cyrus' grotto was shielded from most of the world's sounds by the thick drapery that hung in its entrance. But the recess was so small that Jared had no trouble concentrating on the echoes from his words to hear how much the Thinker had changed.

How fortunate it was the old man had never developed a preference for protecting his face with a curtain of hair. For now he was completely bald. And the wrinkles, deposited by a lifetime of muscular tension to insure closed eyes, were etched even more deeply.

"I was just considering," Cyrus said, explaining his silence, "whether the monster could have purposely left that thing in the entrance. And I'm convinced it did. What do you think?"

"It sounded that way to me."

"What do you suppose its purpose was?"

Jared listened to the fervent supplications of the Litany of Light from the Revitalization Ceremony across the world. Audible, too, was the conversation of his Official Escort, waiting outside to take him to the Upper Level.

"That's one of the things I wanted to talk about," he said finally. "Tell me about—Darkness."

"Darkness?" There was the sound of Cyrus' chin wedging itself between thumb and forefinger. "We used to talk a lot about that, didn't we? What is it you'd like to know?"

"Is it possible Darkness can be connected with"—Jared hesitated—"the eyes?"

After a few beats the other said, "Not that I can hear—not any more than with the knee or little finger. Why do you ask?"

"I figure it might be close to Light in some way or other."

Cyrus weighed the proposition. "Light Almighty—infinite goodness. Darkness—infinite evil, according to the beliefs. The principle of relative opposites. You can't have one without the other. If there were no Darkness, then Light would be everywhere. Yes, I suppose you could say there is a negative relationship. But I don't hear where the eyes would fit into the composite."

Coughing, Jared rose and swayed against the dizzying effects of his fever. "Have you ever felt Effective Excitation?"

"In the Optic Nerve Ceremony? Yes. Many gestations ago."

"Well, in Effective Excitation you're supposed to be feeling Light. And if the existence of Light depends in a negative way on the existence of Darkness, then the eyes must also be designed to feel Darkness."

Jared listened to the other rub his face in deep thought. "Sounds logical," the Thinker conceded.

"If one found Darkness, do you suppose he might also find—"

But Cyrus wouldn't let his running thoughts be repressed. "If we're going to talk about Darkness as a material concept, let's ask ourselves: What *is* Darkness? We find it could—now mind you, I say *could*, because it's just an idea—could be a universal medium. That means it exists everywhere—in the air about us, in the passageways, in the infinite rocks and mud."

Jared's fever turned into a sudden chill, but he kept his attention on the other's words.

"Point number two," Cyrus went on, his voice now reflecting against a second upthrust finger. "If it's so universal then it must be completely undetectable through the senses."

Disappointed, Jared sank back on the bench. If the Thinker were correct, he could *never* expect to find Darkness. "Then why would it exist at all?"

"It might be the medium by which sound is transmitted."

They were both silent awhile.

"No Jared. I don't think you could ever expect to find Darkness anywhere in this universe."

Eagerly, Jared asked, "Would there be less Darkness beyond infinity?"

"If you have our so-called Paradise in mind, then we can forget about Darkness as a *physical* medium. In that case I would say—yes, there must be less Darkness in Paradise since Paradise is supposed to be full of Light."

"What's your composite of Paradise?"

The Thinker laughed. "If you've an ear for the beliefs, you'll have to admit it must have been wonderful. Man was supposed to be godlike. Thanks to the presence everywhere of Light, it was possible to know what lay ahead *without* smelling or hearing it. Nor did we have to go about feeling things. It was as though our senses were all rolled up into one and could be projected many times the distance that even the strongest voice carries."

Jared sat there thinking how uninspiring had been this visit to Cyrus. He hadn't even gotten encouragement in his quest for Light.

"Your Escort's waiting," the Thinker reminded.

"One more question: How do you explain the Optic Nerve Ceremony?"

"I don't know. It bothers me too. And Light knows I've done enough thinking about it. But here's something: Effective Excitation *could* be some sort of normal body function."

"In what way?"

"Close your eyes—*real tight*. Now—what do you hear?"

"There's a roaring noise in my ears."

"Right. Now, suppose for generations we had to live in a place where there was no sound. Nobody now alive would have ever heard anything. But perhaps the legend of sound has been passed down—through a touch language, let's say."

"I don't hear what—"

"Can you imagine that there might now be such a thing as an Excitation of the Hearing Nerve Ceremony? That's what you just did when you tightened your facial muscles. And there might now be a Guardian of the Way who would make you squinch up your face and feel the Great Sound Almighty."

Jared rose excitedly. "Those rings of silent sound we feel during Effective Excitation—you mean they might have a connection with something people once *did* with their eyes?"

He plainly caught Cyrus' shrug as the Thinker said, "I mean nothing. I'm merely posing a theoretical question."

The old man's breathing became shallow with meditation.

Jared stepped toward the curtain, then paused and listened back in the direction of the Thinker. Long ago he had believed he might find less Darkness in the Original World and recognize it for what it was. But Cyrus had concluded Darkness was a universal medium which couldn't be sensed.

Wasn't it possible, however, that Light could have a canceling effect—could *erase* some of the Darkness? And if one were lucky enough to hear the cancellation taking place, might he not get a clue as to the nature of both Light and Darkness?

Then something vastly more important occurred to him: Cyrus had said the presence of Light Almighty in Paradise made it possible for man to "know what lay ahead *without* smelling or hearing it"!

Wasn't that exactly what the Zivvers could do? Was it that the Zivvers, too, shared some peculiar relationship with Light—a relationship which they themselves probably didn't even suspect?

He had already sensed an intrinsic association among Light, Darkness, the eyes, the Original World, and the Twin Devils. Now it seemed he would have to include the Zivvers with that group. For, whenever they zivved, there must be less of something around them as a result of that zivving—just as there was less silence when a normal person listened to noise. And that lessness, in the Zivvers' case, might well be the lessness he was seeking—a lessness of Darkness!

Recalling that Della was a Zivver, he was suddenly anxious to return to the Upper Level so he could keep an ear on her and perhaps hear what there was less of in her vicinity whenever she zivved.

Jared brushed the curtain aside.

"Good-bye, son—and good luck," Cyrus called, then sneezed.

Jared dismissed his Official Escort at the last bend before the entrance to the Upper Level. There would be no need for them to wait for the runner who had come ahead, since it had been decided that the man would remain here for a while.

In a way, he was glad to get rid of the others. The Captain had kept on complaining of a sore throat and another of the crew had coughed so much it was hard to hear the tones of the clickstones.

Moreover, those who had no complaint over personal discomfort had been on edge over the fact that they thought they detected the scent of the monster from time to time. Jared himself could smell nothing—not with his nose stopped up the way it was. Nor could he hear very much, since the general stuffiness in his head seemed to have extended to his ear passages too.

Shivering with a chill, he sounded his stones for maximum volume and staggered on down the passageway, wishing all the while that he'd reported in to the Injury Treatment Grotto instead of going on with Declaration of Unification Intentions.

He rounded the sweeping curve and paused, listening ahead. There was brisk activity up there—rock being cast down on top of rock, methodically but swiftly. Voices—the voices of two men mumbling in desperate tones, swearing and invoking the name of Light Almighty.

Rattling his pebbles more intently, he listened to the *clicks* echo against the men as they darted about collecting rocks and depositing them in a heap against one wall of the Upper Level entrance.

Then he realized he was *hearing silent sound—in front of the pair*! It was attached to the wall.

The small bundle of frozen echoes seemed to be plastered there and the men were frantically covering it up with stones. One of them belatedly heard Jared's presence, shouted fearfully and bolted back into the world.

"It's only Fenton—from the Lower Level," the other called.

But it was audible that the man didn't intend to return.

Jared started forward and drew back, dismayed. Again he was certain the screaming silence wasn't reaching him through his ears. He was *actually* hearing (if that was the word for it) the stuff with his eyes! He proved that much by turning his head the other way; he instantly became altogether unaware of its presence.

When he turned back, the bundle of soundless noise was gone—*completely*. And it seemed significant that he had heard the man put the final rock on the pile, thereby finishing the echo barrier.

"You'd better get inside," the other warned, "before the monster comes back!"

"What happened?"

Reflections of his words fetched a composite of the man raising a trembling hand to wipe perspiration off his face. "The monster didn't take anyone this time. It only stayed out here swabbing the wall with—"

He screamed and shook his head violently in front of him. Then he plunged deafly down the passage, sobbing, "Light Almighty!"

Jared readily heard what had frightened the other. The palm of his hand was full of the roaring silence!

He advanced curiously on the rock pile. But a seizure of coughing drove home the realization of how sick he was and he stumbled on into the Upper Level World.

There was nobody at the entrance to meet him this time, so he used the *clacks* of the central caster to sound his way to the Wheel's grotto. He found Anselm pacing behind the curtain and muttering to himself, grim-voiced and tense.

"Come in, my boy—rather, Prime Survivor," the Wheel invited. "Wish I could say I'm glad to have you back."

He returned to his pacing and Jared dropped miserably down on a bench. He cupped his feverish face in his hands.

"Sorry to hear about your father, my boy. I was shocked when the runner told me. We've had three people taken by the monsters since you left."

"I came back," Jared said weakly, "to Declare Unification In—"

"Unification Intentions—compost!" Anselm boiled over as he faced Jared with hands on his hips. "At a time like this you've got *Unification* on your mind?"

When Jared didn't answer, he said, "Sorry, my boy. But we're on edge up here—with monsters running all over the place and hot springs drying up. Five more boiled out yesterperiod. I understand you've been having the same trouble."

Jared nodded, not particularly caring whether the Wheel heard.

Anselm mumbled some more and said, "Unification! Didn't the runner tell you I'd decided to put things off until we can do something about all these other complications?"

"I haven't heard the runner. Where is he?"

"I sent him back early this period."

Jared slumped on the bench, his body boiling like a turbulent spring. The runner had already left but hadn't reached the Lower Level. And they hadn't passed him on the way up. Only ominous significance could be attached to the fact that several members of the Official Escort—those with clear noses, at least—had told of smelling the lingering scent of the monster in the passageway.

His lungs convulsed in a coughing spell and when he finished he was aware the Adviser had entered the grotto and was standing there listening intensely down at him.

"Well, Fenton," Lorenz said bluntly, "what do *you* make of all this monster business?"

Jared trembled with another chill. "I don't know what to think of it."

"I've told the Wheel what *I* think: The Zivvers have gone back to their old tricks. They're taking Survivors as slaves. And they're in league with the Twin Devils to accomplish their purpose."

"And I say that's ridiculous," put in Anselm. "We even *heard* the monsters take a Zivver!"

"How do we know that wasn't something they *wanted* us to hear?"

Anselm snorted. "If the Zivvers are going to start taking slaves again, they'd just *do* it."

Lorenz was silent. But it was an adamant silence. It was readily audible he was going to insist the monsters and Zivvers were working together. And Jared could understand why: if the Adviser intended to accuse him of being a Zivver, he was going to make certain the accusation also included indirect blame for the presence of the monsters.

"I'm sure Della will want to hear your decision on Unification, my boy." Anselm took the Adviser by the arm and swept the curtain aside. "I'll send her in."

Jared coughed, spanned his steaming forehead with a trembling hand and shivered.

A short while later the girl entered and drew in a sharp breath as she stood with her back against the curtain.

"Jared!" she exclaimed with deep concern. "You're boiling! What's wrong?"

He was surprised at first that she could hear his fever all the way across the grotto. But fever was heat. And heat was the stuff Zivvers zivved, wasn't it?

"I don't know," he managed.

For a moment he had almost generated interest in the fact that she was here and zivving. And that now was his chance to listen closely and perhaps hear whether there was a lessness of something around her *while* she zivved. But his purpose faded away in another jarring shiver.

Della closed the curtain securely behind her and came over. He turned his head and coughed and she knelt before him, feeling the heat in his arms and face. And he heard her features twist with concern.

But she pushed the expression aside for something that was evidently more urgent. "Jared, I'm sure the Adviser knows you're a Zivver!" she whispered. "He hasn't come out and said so, but he keeps reminding everybody how remarkable your senses are!"

Jared swayed forward, caught himself and sat there trembling and perspiring, his head roaring, spinning.

"Don't you hear why he made you shoot at that target among the hot springs?" she went on. "He *knows* what too much heat does to a Zivver! He was just trying to find out if you—"

The girl's words faded into oblivion as he toppled forward off the bench.

When finally he awoke, there was the waning taste in his mouth of medicinal mold and the vague memory of having been forced to swallow the mushy substance several times.

Too, he sensed that during the entire period—or was it longer?—he had lain semiconscious in the Wheel's grotto, Kind Survivoress had tried to force her way back into his delirious dreams. Perhaps she had even succeeded. But he could recall neither her successful intrusion nor the dreams themselves.

Now he felt only an inner calm and comfort. His throat was smooth again and the pounding fever had left his head. Even if he was not entirely well, he felt certain that only a full return of his strength stood in the way of complete recovery.

Gradually, he became aware of restrained breathing at the other end of the grotto and recognized the rhythm and depth of the breaths as Della's.

There was the firm, supple sound of thigh and calf muscles working together as she paced—nervously, he could tell by the erratic steps—to the curtain and back again.

Then she came abruptly over to the slumber ledge and shook him desperately. "Jared, wake up!"

He could tell from the urgency in her voice that she had been trying to arouse him for some time.

"I'm awake."

"Oh, thank Light!" Some of her hair had come out of the band that held it tightly behind her head and had fallen across her face. She brushed it aside and he got a clearer impression of smooth, precise features that were taut with solicitude.

"You've got to get out of here!" she went on in a strained whisper. "The Adviser's convinced Uncle Noris you're a Zivver! They're going to—"

There was the sound of nearby conversation in the outside world and Jared heard the soft current of air swirl around her face as she jerked her head toward the curtain, then back again.

"They're coming!" she warned. "Maybe we can slip out before they get here!"

He tried to rise but fell back down, weak and puzzled, as he suddenly realized the girl didn't customarily bend an ear toward an interesting noise, as everyone else did. She always kept her face pointed directly at anything that held her attention. Which meant she didn't ziv with her ears! But, then, what *did* she ziv with?

The voices outside came more clearly through the curtain now.

Adviser: "Of *course* I'm dead certain he's a Zivver! As good a marksman as he is, he couldn't hit a simple stationary target in the manna orchard. And you know as well as I do that Zivvers are confused by excessive heat."

Wheel: "It *does* seem incriminating."

Adviser: "And what about Aubrey? We sent him out to cover that silent sound the monster left on the wall outside. That was two periods ago and he's been missing ever since. Who was the last one to hear him?"

Wheel, coughing hoarsely: "Byron says that when he ran back into the world, Fenton was still out there with Aubrey."

Adviser, sneezing: "There you are! And if you need any more proof that Fenton's a Zivver who has conspired with the monsters, you have one of our basic beliefs to go by."

Wheel: "The one that says any Survivor who consorts with Cobalt or Strontium will become deathly sick."

They stepped deliberately toward the grotto entrance.

Wheel, with a sniffle: "What'll we do with him?"

Adviser: "The Pit'll hold him for the moment." Another sneeze. "Being a Zivver, he'll be worth something as a hostage, no doubt."

When they drew the curtain aside Jared heard several armed Protectors taking their posts outside the grotto.

Wheel Anselm came and stood beside Jared, edging Della aside. "Has he made any wakeful noises yet?"

"He's not a Zivver!" she pleaded. "Let him alone!"

Jared heard that her face was turned directly toward the Wheel. And again he caught the fleeting impression of her hand brushing hair away from her forehead—away from her eyes, actually.

And now he remembered that just before she had handed him the tubular object the monsters had left behind, she had brought it up before her and held it on a level with her face.

It was her *eyes* that she was zivving with!

Anselm seized his arm and shook him roughly. "All right—up off that ledge! We can hear you're awake!"

Feebly, Jared struggled to his feet. Lorenz seized his other arm, but he shook off the grip.

"Protectors!" the Adviser shouted anxiously.

And the guards hurried in.

CHAPTER EIGHT

ALTHOUGH HE HADN'T THOUGHT IT possible, the Upper Level Punishment Pit was worse than the one in Jared's own world. It occurred to him that it would be hard to imagine a more terrible penalty for wrongdoing. As a detention facility, it was escape-proof. The ledge on which he lay was fully two body lengths below the surface. And it was much narrower than his shoulders, so that an arm and leg had to dangle over the abyss.

Lowered there by rope, he lay motionless for hundreds of heartbeats—until his limbs had become numb. Then, cautiously, he had dropped one of his clickstones into the hole. It had fallen—fallen—fallen. And many breaths later, after he had given up hope of listening to the impact, there was the faintest *kerplunk* he had ever heard.

From remote distances came the sounds of late period activity—children at play after their Familiarization session, manna shells scraping slabs during mealtime, and a staccato frequency of coughs.

Eventually, the echo caster was turned off for the sleep period and, still later, Della came.

On a cord she lowered a shell filled with food. Then she lay with her head overhanging the mouth of the Pit.

"I almost convinced Uncle Noris you couldn't be a Zivver," she whispered disappointedly, "until that epidemic got him excited all over again."

"That sneezing and coughing?"

The steady flow of her voice wavered as she nodded her head. "They ought to be taking mold, like we did. But Lorenz's telling them it won't work against Radiation sickness."

She fell silent and he let the manna shell clatter against the wall of the Pit. Intercepting the sharp echoes, he quickly put together a composite of the girl's features. And even more than before, he liked what he heard.

The general configuration was soft and confident. Her hair, slicked back from her forehead, had a pleasant sound and gave her face a sleek, delicate tonal balance. Somehow the total impression had much in common with the wistful music she had stroked from the hanging stones. And he fully heard now how desirable she was for Unification.

He brought another shelled crayfish to his mouth, but paused when he realized that even now she must be zivving. Again he let the bowl strike rock to produce more sounding echoes. And he heard that her face was directed fixedly toward him. He could almost feel the intense steadiness of her eyes.

Now was hardly the time, though, to listen for whatever happened to the things about her whenever she zivved. If there was a lessening of something or other, he certainly wouldn't be able to detect it while clinging precariously to the ledge.

Nevertheless, he did seize upon one fact that had, at the moment, become clear: since both Darkness and Light were probably connected with the eyes—perhaps especially with a Zivver's eyes—then the lessness he was listening for would no doubt have a measurable effect *on* the eyes.

Wait! There *was* something—back in the Wheel's grotto, when Della had bent over him to shake him awake. Some of her hair had fallen over her face. And when she had brushed it aside, wasn't there then *less hair* before her eyes?

He slumped with a tinge of futility. No—Darkness couldn't be as simple a thing as hair. That would be too ironic—listening for something he had known all his life. Anyway, Cyrus had said Darkness was universal, everywhere. That meant he would have to listen over a broad area, all around the girl.

"Jared," she said tentatively. "You're not—I mean you and the monsters aren't—"

"I haven't had anything to do with them."

Her breath escaped with a relieved sound. "Are you from—the Zivver World?"

"No. I've never been there."

The echoes of his words captured her depressed expression.

"Then you've spent your whole life hiding the fact you're a Zivver—just like me," she said sympathetically.

There was no point in not encouraging her confidence. "It hasn't been easy."

"No, it hasn't. Knowing how much better you can do things, but having to listen to yourself carefully every step of the way so others won't find out what you are."

"I pushed it to a fine point—too fine, I suppose. Otherwise I wouldn't be down here now."

He heard her hand slide down along the side of the Pit, as though reaching out for him. "Oh, Jared! Does it mean as much to you—finding out you're *not* alone? I never guessed anybody else had to go through the same gestations of Radiation and fear that I did—always afraid of being found out at the next step."

He could appreciate the close relationship she must feel for him, the way her loneliness was crying out. And he sensed something within himself straining toward the girl, even though he was no Zivver in need of sympathetic response.

She went on effusively, "I don't understand why you didn't go hunting for the Zivver World long ago. I would have. But I was always afraid I wouldn't find it and would get lost in the passages."

"I wanted to go there too," he lied. And it was beginning to appear that he *could* play the role of a Zivver simply by following her lead. "But I have an obligation to the Lower Level."

"Yes, I know."

"I don't hear—that is, I don't ziv why you didn't join up with the Zivvers during one of their raids," he said.

"Oh, I couldn't do *that*. What if I tried and the Zivvers wouldn't take me? Then everybody would know what I am. I'd be driven into the passages as a Different One!"

89

She rose and stood zivving down into the Pit.

"You're leaving?" he asked.

"Only until I can figure out some way to help you."

"How long do they intend keeping me here?" He tried to change position but succeeded only in almost slipping off the ledge.

"Until the monsters come back. Then Uncle Noris is going to let them know we have you as a hostage."

Listening to her footfalls recede, he was fascinated with the whole range of things that might come out of his association with the girl. Even if Light and Darkness remained elusive, he at least might learn something about this intriguing ability the Zivvers had.

It was past midsleep when Jared, his muscles cramped and aching, finally managed to ease himself into a sitting position. He tapped the manna shell against rock and listened. It wasn't a very wide hole—about two body lengths across, he estimated. And he could hear that, except for the ledge on which he perched, the sides were barren of fissures and outcroppings that might have provided handholds toward the surface.

He brought a knee up against his chest and secured his foot on the shelf. Then, with arms outstretched against the slick wall, he rose bit by bit until he was standing. Slowly, he turned around, pressing his chest against the rock. Reaching overhead, he produced sharp tones by snapping his fingers. And the sudden drop-off in the sound pattern told him that the rim of the Pit was at least another arm's length beyond his extended hand.

He remained in that position for several hundred beats before he heard all Radiation breaking loose above. Until then there had been only the normal sounds of a world lying dormant in midslumber, with an occasional outburst of coughs ruffling the relative quiet.

Then everything seemed to boil over into a great excitement and confusion as one of the Protectors sounded the fearful warning, "Monsters! Monsters!"

Hoarse shouts, screams, and the audible agitation of people scurrying frenziedly about poured down the Pit.

Jared almost lost his balance as he tilted his head back and became aware that the entire opening above was whispering with silent sound. Unlike the sensation experienced during Effective Excitation, however, there was only one circle of the weird monster stuff. And it didn't seem to be actually touching his eyes. Rather, it corresponded in size and shape with his audible impression of the Pit's mouth.

He tottered on the ledge, flailing his arms to keep from falling, then stood with his face pressed firmly against stone as he listened to someone running in his direction.

In the next instant Jared recognized the Adviser's voice coming from halfway across the world, "You at the Pit yet, Sadler?"

There was another distant outburst of screams as Sadler drew to a halt overhead. "I'm here!" He thudded his spear against rock to sound out Jared's position on the ledge below.

This time it was the Wheel's voice that rose in challenge to the monsters: "We've got Fenton! We know he's working with you! Get back or we'll kill him!"

Another wave of screams suggested that the monsters were ignoring Anselm's threat.

"All right, Sadler," Lorenz roared. "Send him to the bottom!"

The spear tip grazed Jared's shoulder and he winced, sidling along the ledge. It came back again, slipped between his chest and the wall of the Pit and began prying him from his perch. Jared toppled over backward and his arms threshed air as he fought to keep from plunging into the unfathomable abyss.

His flailing hand touched and gripped the lance. He jerked himself desperately upright. He gave the spear a violent tug and the full weight of the man at the other end came along with it.

Abruptly the spear was free in his hand and he felt the rush of air as Sadler went plunging by, screaming all the way down.

The weapon was more than long enough to span the Pit. Jared used it as a prodding stick to locate a minor recess in the opposite side. Wedging its butt into the depression, he propped the point against the wall above him.

Panic subsided as quickly as it had broken out overhead. Apparently the invaders had accomplished their purpose and withdrawn.

Jared hoisted himself onto the wedged spear, reached up, gained a purchase on the lip of the Pit and pulled himself out.

"Jared! You're free!"

Echoes from her footfalls brought fragmentary impressions of Della racing toward him. And he could hear the soft *swish* of the coil of rope slung across her shoulder and brushing against her arm.

He tried to get his bearings. But the residual din of dismayed voices was too confusing to indicate which way the entrance lay.

Della caught his hand. "I couldn't find a rope until just now."

Impulsively, he started off in the direction he was facing.

"No." She spun him around. "The entrance is *this* way. Ziv it?"

"Yes. I ziv it now."

He hung back slightly, letting her remain a step or two ahead and following the tug of her hand.

"We'll circle wide, along by the river," she proposed. "Maybe we can reach the passage before they turn on the central caster."

And he had been hoping someone *would* do just that. Of course he hadn't realized that the *clacks* which would sound out the obstacles before him would also betray their presence to the others.

His foot contacted a minor outcropping and he stumbled. Eventually righting himself with the girl's help, he limped on. Then, constraining the anxiety of escape, he composed himself and called upon all the devices he had acquired through gestations of training when he had to learn to detect the subtle rhythm of a heartbeat, the swishing silence of a lazy stream agitated by the motion of a fish beneath its calm surface, the distant scent and slither of a salamander as it crossed moist stone.

More confident now, he listened for sound—*any* kind of sound, remembering that even the most insignificant noise is useful. There! That lurching catch in Della's breath as she drew in the next lungful of air. It meant she was stepping onto a slight elevation. He was prepared when he reached the rise.

He listened intently to the other things about her. Heartbeats were too indistinct to be useful except as direct sound. But there was something rattling faintly in her carrying case. He sniffed the imperceptible odors of a variety of edibles. She had packed a good deal of food and one morsel was striking the side of her pouch with each step. The slight *flops* meant echoes, if he listened attentively enough. There they were now—almost lost among the greater noises from the rest of the world. But they were sufficiently vivid to relay audible impressions of the things before him.

Now he was sure of himself again.

They left the bank of the river, cutting across behind the manna orchard, and had made it almost to the entrance when someone finally turned on the central echo caster.

Immediately, he caught the full composite of a few faint impressions that had worried him for the last few beats—a guard had just arrived to take his post at the entrance.

A moment later the man sounded the alarm. "Somebody's trying to get out! Two of them!"

Jared lowered his shoulder and charged. He crashed into the sentry, knocking him breathless and bowling him over.

Della caught up with him and they lunged into the passageway. He let her stay in the lead until they had rounded the first bend. Then he produced a pair of stones and pushed ahead of her.

"Clickstones?" she asked, puzzled.

"Of course. If we run into somebody from the Lower Level they might wonder why I'm *not* using them."

"Oh. Jared, why don't we—no. I suppose not."

"What were you going to say?" He felt perfectly at ease now, with the familiar tones of the pebbles faithfully bringing back true impressions of all the hazards ahead.

"I started to say let's go to the Zivver World where we belong."

He pulled up sharply. The Zivver World! Why not? If he was listening for a lessness of something that resulted from zivving, what better place to detect it than in a world where *plenty* of people were doing a *lot* of zivving? But could he get away with it? Could he successfully pose as a Zivver in a world full of Zivvers—and hostile ones at that?

"I can't leave the Lower Level just now," he decided finally.

"That's what I figured. Not with all the trouble they're having. But someperiod, Jared—*someperiod* we'll go there?"

"Someperiod."

She tightened her grip on his hand. "Jared! What if the Wheel sends a runner to the Lower Level to tell them you're a Zivver?"

"They wouldn't—" He paused. He'd started to say they wouldn't believe it. But with the Guardian dedicated to stirring up sentiment against him, he wondered.

When they reached his world, he found it odd that there were no longer any Protectors at the entrance. The clear, firm *clacks* of the central caster did reveal, however, the presence of *some-one* standing there at the end of the passageway. And when he moved closer he received the reflected impression of feminine form, hair-over-face.

It was Zelda.

Hearing them she started. Then, nervously, she probed them with clickstones until they came into the full sound of the caster.

"You sure picked a Radiation of a time to bring a Unification partner back," she reproved after she had recognized Jared.

"Why?"

"There've been two more kidnappings by the monsters," she answered. "That's why we're not defending the entrance any longer. They took one of the Protectors. Meanwhile, the Guardian's managed to get the whole world worked up against you."

"Maybe I can do something about that," he returned irately.

"I don't think you can. You're not Prime Survivor any longer. Romel's taken over." Zelda coughed several times and it sent the hair flying from in front of her face.

He strode off toward the Official Grotto.

"Wait," the girl called. "There's something else. Everybody's boiling at you. Hear all that?"

He listened toward the residential section. The world was re-sounding with coughs.

"They blame you for this epidemic," she explained, "since they remember you were the first to have all the symptoms."

"Jared's back!" someone in the orchard shouted.

Another Survivor, farther along the way, took up the cry and passed it on to still a third.

Presently a score of persons could be heard filing out of the orchard where they had been working. Others spilled from the grottoes. And they were all converging on the entrance.

Jared studied the reflected *clacks* and picked up impressions of Romel and Guardian Philar in the forefront of the advance. They were flanked on either side by a number of Protectors.

Della seized his arm anxiously. "Maybe it would be safer if we just left."

"We can't let *Romel* get away with this."

Zelda added with a crisp laugh, "If you think this world's in a mess now, wait till you hear what Romel does to it."

Jared stood his ground before the approaching Survivors. If he was going to convince them Romel and Philar had merely taken advantage of them in the interest of personal ambition, it would have to be from a position of confidence and dignity.

His brother drew up before him and warned, "If you stay here you're going to hear things my way. I'm Prime Survivor now."

"How did the Elders vote on that?" Jared asked calmly.

"They haven't yet. But they will!" Romel seemed to be losing some of his self-assurance. He paused to listen and make certain he still had the support of the Survivors, who had drawn into a half circle about the entrance.

"No Prime Survivor can be removed," Jared recited the law, "without full hearing."

Guardian Philar stepped forward. "As far as we're concerned, you've *had* your hearing—before a Power more just than any of us, before the Great Light Almighty Himself!"

One of the Survivors shouted, "You've got Radiation sickness! That only comes from having truck with Cobalt or Strontium!"

"And you passed it on to everybody else!" another added, coughing spasmodically.

Jared started to protest, but was promptly shouted down.

And the Guardian said severely, "There are only two sources of Radiation sickness. Either you *did* have something to do with the Twin Devils, as Romel suggested, or the disease is a punishment from Light for your profanity, as I suspect."

It was Jared who was losing his composure now. "It's not true! Ask Cyrus whether I—"

"The monster got Cyrus yesterperiod."

"The Thinker—gone?"

Della tugged on his arm and whispered, "We'd better get out of here, Jared."

There were the sounds of clickstones and running feet in the passageway and he bent an ear to hear who was approaching.

By his pace, it was clear that the man was an official runner. And, when he broke his stride, it was further evident that he had sensed the congestion of persons at the entrance. He halted, then came forward more slowly, and without benefit of stones, to join them.

"Jared Fenton's a Zivver!" he disclosed. "He led the monsters to the Upper Level!"

The Protectors, most of them armed with spears, spread out and encircled Jared and the girl.

Then someone shouted, "Zivvers—in the passage!"

More than half the Survivors turned and fled noisily back toward their grottoes as Jared picked up the scent drifting in from the passageway. Someone redolent with the odors of the Zivver World was approaching—stumbling, falling, rising, and coming forward again.

The Protectors broke ranks as they jockeyed in confusion. The pair nearest the entrance drew back their spears.

Just then the Zivver staggered into the direct sound of the central caster and collapsed on the ground.

"Wait!" Jared shouted, casting himself at the two Protectors who were about to hurl their lances.

"It's only a child!" Della exclaimed.

Jared made his way to the girl, who was groaning with pain. It was Estel, whom he had returned to the Zivver party in the Main Passage.

He heard Della kneel on the other side of the child and run her hands over the girl's chest. "She's hurt! I can feel four or five broken ribs!"

Still, Estel recognized him and he caught the sound of her weak smile. He could sense, too, the animation in her eyes as he listened to them dart up and down in purposeful motion.

"You told me someperiod I'd start zivving—when I least expected it," she managed painfully.

Spear touched spear somewhere behind him and the echoes captured the grimace that twisted the child's smile.

"You were right," she continued feebly. "I was trying to find your world and I fell into a pit. When I climbed out again, I started zivving."

Her head slumped against his arm and he felt the life shudder out of her body.

"Zivver! Zivver!" The incriminating cry rose behind him.

"Jared's a Zivver!"

He seized Della's hand and lunged into the tunnel as two spears struck the wall beside him. He paused only long enough to snatch up the lances, then continued on into the passageway.

CHAPTER NINE

HALF A PERIOD LATER, WITH long stretches of unfamiliar passages behind them, Jared paused and listened tensely.

There it was again! A distant flutter of wings—much too faint for Della's ears, though.

"Jared, what *is* it?" She pressed close against him.

Casually, he said, "I thought I heard something."

Actually, he had suspected for some time that the soubat was trailing them.

"Maybe it's one of the Zivvers!" she suggested eagerly.

"That's what I hoped at first. But I was mistaken. There's nothing there." No sense in alarming her—not just yet.

As long as he could keep the conversation going, he had little to worry about insofar as pitfalls were concerned. The words provided a steady source of sounding echoes. But subject matter was not inexhaustible and eventually there came lapses into silence. It was then that he had to resort to artifice to keep the girl from discovering he wasn't a Zivver. An ingeniously timed cough, an ostensibly awkward clatter of the lances, an unnecessary scuff that sent a loose stone rattling along the ground—all these improvisations helped.

He let a spear strike rock and was rewarded with the reflected composite of a bend in the corridor. As he negotiated it, Della warned. "Watch out for that hanging stone!"

Her alarmed words fetched him an impression of the sliver of rock in all its audible clarity. But too late.

Clop!

The impact of his head snapped the needle in two and sent fragments hurtling against the wall.

"Jared," she asked, puzzled, "aren't you zivving?"

He feigned a groan to avoid answering—not that the instant swelling on his forehead wasn't justification enough for the expression of pain.

"Are you hurt?"

"No." He pushed forward briskly.

"And you aren't zivving either."

He tensed. Had she guessed already? Was he about to lose his only means of entry into the Zivver World?

Even convinced that he wasn't zivving, however, she only laughed. "You're having the same trouble I did—until I said, 'To Radiation with what people think! I'm going to ziv all I want!'"

Using the reflections of her clearly enunciated syllables, he planted firmly in mind the details of the area immediately ahead. "You're right. I wasn't zivving."

"We don't have to deny our ability any longer, Jared." She held on to his arm. "That's all behind us now. We can be ourselves for the first time—really ourselves! Oh, isn't it wonderful?"

"Sure." He rubbed the lump on his forehead. "It's wonderful."

"That girl who was waiting for you at the Lower Level—"

"Zelda?"

"What an odd name—and a fuzzy-face too. Was she a—friend?"

At least the echo-generating conversation was under way again. And now he could readily hear all the obstacles.

"Yes, I suppose you'd call her a friend."

"A *good* friend?"

He led her confidently around a shallow pit, half-expecting a complimentary *"Now* you're zivving!" But it didn't come.

"Yes, a good friend," he said.

"I gathered as much—from the way she was waiting for you."

With his head turned away, he smiled. Zivvers, it appeared, were not lacking in normal human sensitivity. And he felt somewhat gratified over the pout-formed distortion of her words when she asked, "Are you going to—miss her much?"

Hiding his amusement, he offered bravely, "I think I'll manage to get over it."

He faked another cough and detected a vague hollowness lurking in the rebounding sound. Fortunately, he kicked a loose stone with his next step. Its crisp clatter betrayed the details of a chasm that stretched halfway across the corridor.

Della warned, "Ziv that—"

"I ziv it!" he shot back, leading her around the hazard.

After a while she said distantly, "You had lots of friends, didn't you?"

"I don't think I was ever lonesome." He regretted the statement immediately, suspecting that a Zivver in his position more logically *would* have been lonesome—dissatisfied with his lot.

"Not even knowing you were—different from all the others?"

"What I meant," he hastened to explain, "was that most of the people were so nice I could almost forget I wasn't like them."

"You even knew that poor Zivver child," she added thoughtfully.

"Estel. I only heard—zivved her once before." He told her about encountering the runaway girl in the corridor.

When he had finished she asked, "And you let Mogan and the others get away without even telling them you were a Zivver too?"

"I—that is—" He swallowed heavily.

"Oh," she said with belated comprehension, "I forgot—you had your friend Owen with you. And he would have heard your secret."

"That's right."

"Anyway, you couldn't desert the Lower Level, knowing how much they needed you."

He listened suspiciously at her. Why had she been so quick to provide the answers for which he had been only groping? It was as though she had whimsically put him on a hook, then deftly taken him off again. Did she *know* he was no Zivver? Somehow it seemed his entire plan to investigate the possible Zivver-Darkness-Eyes-Light relationship might be slipping into an obscure echo void.

Again he was jarred from his thoughts by the portentous sound of fanning wings—still too distant for Della to detect.

Without slowing his pace, he concentrated on the ominous flapping. There were two of the beasts trailing them now!

The logical thing to do, he readily heard, would be to dig in and face the soubats promptly—before they attracted others to the pursuit. He held off with the hope that the passage would narrow sufficiently to let him and the girl through but not the soubats.

He slowed his pace and waited for Della to say something so there would be more sounding echoes.

Clop!

The impact of shoulder against hanging stone wasn't quite as jolting this time. It merely spun him half-around.

Angered, he snatched a pair of clickstones out of his pouch and rattled them furiously. To Radiation with what she thought! If the truth that he wasn't a Zivver was going to come out, let it come!

Della only laughed. "Go ahead and use your stones if it'll make you feel any more secure. I went through the same thing when I first started zivving steadily."

"You did?" He stepped off at a brisk pace now that what lay ahead was so sharply audible.

"You'll soon get used to it. It's the air currents that cause all the trouble. They're beautiful but tiring."

Currents? Did that mean there was some way she could be aware of slow, swirling air in the corridor—something *he* could *hear* only when it was further agitated by the passage of a spear or arrow?

It was Della who tripped this time. She fell against him, throwing them both off balance and sending them reeling against the wall.

She clung to him and he could feel the moist warmth of her breath on his chest, the cleaving softness of her body against his.

He held her for a moment and she whispered, "Oh, Jared— we're going to be *so* happy! No two people ever had more in common!"

Her cheek was smooth where it pressed against his shoulder and her banded tress of hair lay softly across his arm, dancing as it moved with the slight motions of her head.

Dropping his spears, he touched her face and felt the even flow of trim features, firm and fine from hairline to chin. Her waist, molded to the concavity of his other hand, was evenly curved and supple, flaring out to modestly rounded hips.

Not until then had he fully realized she might quite easily become more than just a means to an end. And he was certain he had been wrong in suspecting she was trying to deceive him—so certain that he found himself thinking of forgetting everything else and settling down with her in some remote, lesser world.

But sobering logic barged in on his reverie and he retrieved the lances abruptly, shoving off down the passage. Della was a Zivver; he wasn't. She would find happiness in her Zivver World and he would have to be content with his quest for Light—if he managed to survive his bold invasion of the Zivver domain.

"Are you zivving now, Della?" he asked cautiously.

"Oh, I ziv all the time. Soon you will too."

Experimentally, he listened sharply with the faint hope that he would notice some indiscernible change in the things about her. But he heard nothing. It must be as he had previously suspected: the lessness he sought was so minor that he would have to be in the presence of a number of Zivvers before its cumulative effect would be noticeable.

But, wait! There was a more direct approach.

"Della, tell me—what do you think about Darkness?"

And he could hear her echo-conveyed frown as she repeated the question and added uncertainly, "Darkness abounds in the worlds—"

"Sin and evil, no doubt."

"Of course. What else?"

It was evident she knew nothing of Darkness. Or, even if she could perceive it, she still didn't recognize it for what it was.

"Why are you so concerned over Darkness?" she asked.

"I was just thinking," he improvised, "that zivving must be something opposite to Darkness—something good."

"Of course it's good," she assured, following him around a lesser depression and along the shore of a suddenly emerged river. "How could anything so beautiful be bad?"

"It's—beautiful?" He tried to eliminate the questioning inflection at the last beat. But, still, the words came out more interrogation than statement.

Her voice was animate with expressiveness. "That rock up ahead—ziv how it stands out against the cool earth background, how warm and soft it is. Now it's not there, but just for a beat—until that breath of warm air goes by. Now it's back again."

His mouth hung open. How could the rock be there and not there in the next instant. It had continued to cast back *clicks* from his stones all the while, hadn't it? Why, it hadn't moved even a finger's width!

The passage, he could hear, was wide and straight, with few hazards. So he put his stones away.

"You're zivving now, aren't you, Jared? What do you ziv?"

He hesitated. Then, impulsively, "Out there in the stream—I ziv a fish. A big one, standing out against the cool river bed."

"How can *that* be?" she asked skeptically. "*I* can't ziv it."

But certainly it was there! He could hear the swishing of its fins as it stabilized itself. "It's there, all right."

"But a fish is no colder or warmer than the water around it. Besides, I've never been able to ziv rocks or anything else in water—not even when I've just thrown them in."

Covering over the blunder would call for boldness. "*I* can ziv fish. Maybe I ziv different from you."

She was audibly concerned. "I hadn't thought of that. Oh, Jared, suppose I'm not really a Zivver after all!"

"You're a Zivver, all right." Then he lapsed into a troubled silence. How could anyone expect to outsmart a Zivver?

The fearsome rustle of leathery wings overtook him and he marveled that anything that distinct could escape the girl's attention. The creatures had reached an enlarged stretch of the passage and, making the most of ample flying room, were streaking forward.

Then he pulled up and trained his ears acutely on the rearward sounds. No longer were there only two soubats stalking them. It was clearly audible that their number had at least doubled.

"What is it, Jared?" Della questioned his alert silence.

One of the creatures filled the air with its strident cry.

"Soubats!" she exclaimed.

"Just one." No point in alarming her when, with a little luck, they might lose the beasts entirely. "You take the lead. I'll bring up the rear—in case it gets in position to attack."

He prided himself on having worked a temporary advantage out of the situation. With her in front, he no longer had to prove occasionally that he was zivving. Now, with her hand in his, he had only to follow her lead. Still, vocal sounds were even more desirable for fetching obscure impressions, so he primed the conversation.

"Leading me by the hand like this," he offered facetiously, "you remind me of Kind Survivoress."

"Who's that?"

Trailing Della along a ridge that ran beside the stream, he told her of the woman who, in his childhood dreams, used to take him to visit the child who lived with her.

"Little Listener?" she repeated the name after he mentioned it. "That's what the boy was called?"

"In my dreams it was. He couldn't hear anything except the soundless noises some of the crickets made."

"If they were soundless, how did you know the crickets were making any noise at all?" She led him over a minor chasm.

"As I remember, the woman used to tell me such noises existed but only the boy could hear them. She heard them too whenever she listened into his mind, however."

"She could do *that?*"

"Without strain." His chuckle made it clear that he was merely poking fun at the absurdity of his imagination. "That's how she was able to reach me. I remember how she used to say she could listen in on almost anybody's mind anywhere—except a Zivver's."

Della paused beside a rock column. *"You're* a Zivver. She reached *your* mind. How do you account for that?"

There! He'd stumbled over his tongue again. And at a time when he was merely making conversation so he could hear the way. But he recovered instantly. "Oh, I was also the only *Zivver* whose mind she could hear. Don't take this too seriously. Dreams don't have to follow logical patterns."

She led the way into a broader stretch of passage. "Parts of yours did."

"What do you mean?"

"Suppose I told you I knew of a baby who never listened in the direction of a voice, but whenever his mother caught him listening at the wall, she always found a cricket clinging there."

Somehow that had a familiar ring. "Was there such a baby?"

"In the Upper Level—before I was born."

"What happened to him?"

"They decided he was a Different One. He was let out in the passages before he was even four gestations old."

Now he dimly remembered how his parents used to tell him the same story about the Different child of the Upper Level.

"What are you thinking about, Jared?"

He was silent a long while. Then he laughed. "About how I finally understand why I used to dream about a Little Listener. Don't you hear? I had actually been told about such a person. But the memory stayed below the surface."

"And your—Kind Survivoress?"

Another curtain parted on the sounds of forgotten memory. "Now I can even recall hearing the story of a Different One who had been banished from the Lower Level gestations before I was born—a girl who always seemed to know what other people were thinking!"

"There." Della continued on around a bend. "Now you have your odd dreams all explained."

Almost. Left now to be determined was only the psychological origin of the Forever Man in his imaginings.

He turned his attention ahead and listened to a distant, vast hollowness that enveloped the roar of a cataract. They were nearing the end of the passage and ahead, he was certain, lay a huge world—the Zivver World? He doubted it, for he had long ago lost the scent of Zivvers.

"It's horrible," Della said pensively, "the way people just banish Different Ones."

"The first Zivver was a Different One." He swung back into the lead, using his clickstones. "But when they banished him he was old enough to steal back for a Unification partner."

They broke out of the passage and Jared listened to the river flowing on across level ground, headed for the far wall. He shouted and the trailing echoes plunged back down from tremendous heights and across forbidding distances. The words rebounded from grotesque islands of tumbled rocks, setting up a clashing dissonance.

"Jared, it's beautiful!" the girl exclaimed, turning her head in all directions. "I've never zivved anything like *this* before!"

"We can't lose any time reaching the other side," he said calmly. "There should be another passage where the stream flows into the opposite wall."

"That soubat?" she asked, detecting the concern in his voice.

Without answering, he led her swiftly along a level course that had been eroded to smoothness during times past when the river had been fuller than it was now. Many breaths later they plunged through the passageway entrance in the opposite wall— just as the pursuing creatures emerged from the tunnel behind them and hurtled forward, filling the world with their malevolent stridency.

"We've got to hide!" he shouted. "They'll overtake us in a beat!"

They splashed through a bend in the river and echoes of the sound betrayed the presence of an opening in the left wall barely large enough to admit them. He followed Della through and found himself in a recess almost as small as a residential grotto. The girl dropped exhausted to the ground and Jared settled down beside her, listening to the enraged soubats congregating in the corridor outside.

Della rested her head on his shoulder. "Do you think we'll *ever* find the Zivver World?"

"Why are you so anxious to get there?"

"I—well, maybe for the same reason you are."

Of course, she *couldn't* know his real reason—or, could she? "It's where we belong, isn't it?"

"More than that, Jared. You sure you're not going there to—find some people too?"

"What people?"

She hesitated. "Your relatives."

His brow knitted. "I have no relatives there."

"Then I suppose you must be an *original* Zivver."

"Isn't that what you are?"

"Oh, no. You see, I'm a—spur." And she quickly added, "Does that make any difference—between us, I mean?"

"Why, no." But even that sounded too stuffy. "Radiation, no!"

"I'm glad, Jared." She brushed her cheek against his arm. "Of course, nobody knew I was a spur except my mother."

"She was a Zivver too?"

"No. My father was."

He listened outside the recess. Frustrated, the shrieking soubats were beginning to withdraw to the world they had just left.

"But I don't understand," he told the girl.

"It's simple." She shrugged. "After my mother found out I was going to be born, she Unified with an Upper Level Survivor. Everybody thought I just came early."

"You mean," he asked delicately, "your mother and—a Zivver—"

"Oh, it wasn't like that. They wanted to be Unified. They met accidentally in a passageway once—and many times after that. They finally decided to run off together, find a small world of their own. On the way, though, she fell part way down a pit and he got killed saving her. There was nothing else she could do except return to the Upper Level."

Jared felt a keen compassion for the girl. And he could understand how fervently she must have longed for the Zivver World. He had placed his arm around her and drawn her comfortably close. But now he released her, acutely aware of the distinction between them. It was more than the mere physical difference between a Zivver and a non-Zivver. It was a great chasm

107

of divergent thought and philosophy that encompassed contrary values and standards. And he could almost grasp the disdain a Zivver would feel for anyone to whom zivving was only an incomprehensible function.

There were no more soubats in the corridor, so he said, "We'd better get on our way."

But she only sat there, rigid and not breathing. And, momentarily, he imagined he heard some faint, scurrying sounds that he hadn't noticed before. To make certain, he rattled his pebbles. Immediately he received the impression of many small, furry forms. Now he could hear the feather-soft touch of insect feet against stone.

Della screamed and sprang up. "Jared, this is a *spider* world! I've just been bitten on the arm!"

Even as they ran for the exit he heard her falter in stride. As she collapsed, he caught her in his arms and shoved her into the corridor, crawling through after her. But too late. One of the tiny, hairy things had already dropped onto his shoulder. And before he could brush it off he felt the sharp, boiling sting of lethal venom.

Clinging to his lances, he slung Della over his shoulder and stumbled on down the passage. The poison was coursing through his arm now and reaching torturously across his chest, into his head.

But he pushed on for more than one impelling reason: he couldn't lose consciousness here—the soubats would be back at any moment; nor could there be any stopping until he reached a hot spring where he might fashion steaming poultices and tend their wounds.

He struck a rock, bounced off, stood swaying for a while, then staggered on. Around the next bend he waded through an arm of the river and collapsed when he reached dry land again.

The stream flowed off through the wall and before them stretched a broad, dry passage. Pulling himself forward with the hand that still clutched the spears, he dragged Della along with him. Then he paused, listening to a *drip-drip* that came with a melodious monotony. His spear point touched rock and the *thunk* provided him with a composite of the passageway.

It was a strangely familiar corridor, with its slender hanging stone dripping cold water into the puddle below, not too far away from a single, well-defined pit. He felt sure he had been here many times before; had stood beside that moist needle of rock and run his hands over its cool, slick contours.

And, in his last impression before he lapsed into unconsciousness, he recognized all the details of the passageway outside the imaginary world of Kind Survivoress.

CHAPTER TEN

JARED FLINCHED FROM THE ABSURD impressions, from the contradictory composites of physical orientation. He was certain he still lay in the corridor near the dripping needle of rock. Yet, he was equally sure he was somewhere else.

The drip-drip *of the water changed to a weary* tap-tap-tap *and back to a* drip-drip *again. The coarse hardness of stone under his feverish body was, alternately, the soft fibers of manna husks piled upon a sleeping ledge.*

In the next phase of the here-there alternation, the distant tap-tap-tap *commanded his attention. And its sharp echoes conveyed the impression of someone seated on a ledge absently drumming his finger on stone.*

Light, but the man was old! *Had it not been for the movement of his hand, he might easily have been mistaken for a skeleton. The head, trembling with an affliction of senility, was like a skull. And the beard, unkempt and sparse, trailed to the ground, losing itself in the inaudibility of its thinness.*

Tap-tap-tap ... drip-drip ...

Jared was back in the corridor. And, like commingling sounds, the straggly beard had metamorphosed into the moist hanging stone.

"Relax, Jared. Everything's under control now."

He almost lurched out of the dream. "Kind Survivoress!"

"It'll be less awkward if you just call me Leah."

He puzzled over the name, then thought flatly, "I'm dreaming again."

110

"For the moment—yes."

Another anxious, soundless voice intruded, "Leah! How's he doing?"

"Coming around," she said.

"So I can hear." Then, *"Jared?"*

Jared, however, had returned to the corridor—but only for a moment. Soon he was back on the manna fiber mattress in a minor world where the vague outline of a woman bent over him and an inconceivably ancient man sat against the far wall tapping his finger.

"Jared," the woman offered, *"that* other voice *was Ethan's."*

"Ethan?"

"You knew him as Little Listener before we changed his name. He's been out after game, but he's coming back now."

Jared was even more confused.

More to soothe him than for any other reason, he felt sure, the woman said, "I can't believe you found your way here after all these gestations."

He started to say something, but she interrupted, "Don't explain. I heard everything from your mind—what you were doing in the passages, how you were bitten by—"

"Della!" he shouted, remembering.

"She'll be all right. I reached you in time."

Abruptly, he realized he was awake now and that Kind Survivoress' last words had been spoken.

"Not Kind Survivoress, Jared—Leah."

And he was astonished by his audible impression of the woman. He sent his hands groping over her face, across her shoulders, along her arms. Why—she wasn't the least bit old!

"What did you expect—someone like the Forever Man?" She sent her thoughts to him. *"After all, I was really practically a child when I used to go to you."*

He listened more closely at her. Hadn't she once told him she could reach his mind only when he was asleep?

"Only when you're asleep if you're far away," she clarified. "When you're this close you don't have to be asleep."

He studied her auditory reflections. She was perhaps a bit taller than Della. But her proportions, despite her nine or ten gestations' seniority over the girl, suffered none in comparison.

She was closed-eyed and kept her hair clipped shoulder-length on the sides, reaching to her eyebrows in front.

Turning his ears on his surroundings, he listened to a small, dismal world with a scattering of hot springs, each surrounded by its usual clump of manna plants; an arm of a river flowing out of and right back into the wall; another slumber ledge nearby—Della there, asleep. All these impressions he sifted from the echoes provided by the finger tapping of—the Forever Man?

"That's right," Leah confirmed.

He rose, feeling not as weak as he thought he would, and started across the world.

Leah cautioned, "We don't disturb him until he stops tapping."

He came back and stood in front of the woman, still rejecting the fact that he was actually *here,* in his preposterous dream setting. "How did you know I was out in the corridor?"

"I listened to you coming." And he heard the unspoken explanation that *listen,* in this case, didn't mean hearing *sound.*

She placed a solicitous hand on his shoulder. "And I also hear from your thoughts that this Della is a Zivver."

"She thinks I'm one too."

"Yes, I know. And I'm afraid. I don't understand what you're trying to do."

"I—"

"Oh, I know what you have in mind. But I still don't understand it. I realize you want to get to the Zivver World so you can hunt for Darkness."

"For Light too. And using Della is the only way I can get in."

"So I hear. But how do you know what *her* plans are? I don't trust the girl, Jared."

"It's just because you can't listen to what she's thinking."

"Maybe that's it. Maybe I'm so used to hearing feelings, intentions, that I'm lost when outer impressions are all I have to go by."

"You won't tell Della I'm not like her?"

"If that's the way you want it. We'll just let her go on believing you're the only Zivver whose mind I can reach. But I hope you know what you're doing."

112

Little Listener came storming into the world and it was remarkable that his exuberant shouts failed to rouse Della and were ignored by the Forever Man, who merely continued his tapping.

"Jared! Where are you?"

"Over here!" Jared was suddenly swept up in the excitement of renewing an acquaintance he hadn't even known was real.

"He can't hear you—remember?" Leah reminded.

"But he's running straight toward us!" Then he puzzled over the scent of—crickets?—that was coming from Little Listener.

"Ethan," Leah corrected. "And those *are* crickets. He keeps a pouch filled with them. Unhearable cricket noises make just as good echoes for him as clickstones do for you."

Then the other was upon him and, in a bone-crushing embrace, swung him around and around as easily as he would a bundle of manna stalks.

Jared's gratification over the reunion was dulled by his awed appreciation of Ethan's tremendous proportions. It was just as well that Little Listener had been banished from the Upper Level because of his uncanny hearing. Otherwise, he most certainly would have been expelled later for his almost inhuman size.

"You old son of a soubat!" Ethan chortled. "I knew you'd come some period!"

"Light, but it's good to—" Jared broke off in mid-sentence as blunt, trembling fingers came to rest lightly against his lips.

"Let him," Leah urged. "That's the only way he can find out what you're saying."

They spent the better part of a period talking about their childhood meetings. And Jared had to tell them about the worlds of man, how it felt to live with many people, what the Zivvers' latest tricks were, whether there had been any more Different Ones recently.

They interrupted their session once to haul food from a boiling pit and bring a portion to the Forever Man. But the latter, still not talkatively disposed, ignored their presence.

Later, Jared said in answer to Leah's question, "Why do I want to go to the Zivver World? Because I've got a hunch that's the right place to hunt for Darkness and Light."

Ethan shook his head. "Forget it. You're here; stay here."

"No. This is something I've *got* to do."

"Great flying soubats!" the other exclaimed. "You never had ideas like that before!"

At this point Jared, from the edge of his hearing, caught the impression of Della stirring on her ledge.

He hurried over and knelt beside her. He felt her face and it was cool and dry, signifying that she had slept off the fever.

"Where are we?" she asked weakly.

He started to tell her, but before he got halfway through he heard that she had drifted into normal sleep.

During the next period Della more than made up for her inactivity of the previous one. That she had been pensively silent on hearing Jared explain about the world they were in and on meeting Leah and Ethan was a prelude to something or other.

When they were alone later, kneeling beside a hot spring and applying fresh poultices to their spider bites, he learned the reason for her reticence.

"When was the last time you were here?" she demanded.

"Oh, so many gestations ago that I—"

"Manna sauce!" She turned away and the Forever Man's tapping sounds blunted themselves against the cool stiffness of her back. "I must say, your Kind Survivoress is *quite* a surprise."

"Yes, she—" Then he understood what she was intimating.

"Kind Survivoress—I'll *bet* she was kind!"

"You don't think—"

"Why did you bring me along? Was it because you thought that awkward giant might be interested in a Unification partner?"

Then she relented. "Oh, Jared, have you forgotten about the Zivver World already?"

"Of course not."

"Then let's get on our way."

"You don't understand. I can't just run off. Leah saved our lives. These are friends!"

"Friends!" She cleared her throat and made it sound like the lash of a swish-rope. "You and your friends!"

Her head insolently erect, she strode off.

Jared followed, but drew up sharply when the world was suddenly cast into silence.

The Forever Man had stopped tapping! He was ready for company!

Unaccountably hesitant, Jared advanced cautiously across the world. Leah and Ethan had been credible. But the Forever Man loomed like a haunting creature from a fantastic past—someone whom he could never hope to understand.

Orienting himself by the asthmatic rasps that came from ahead, he approached the ledge.

"This is Jared," Leah's unspoken introduction rippled the psychic silence. *"He's finally come to hear us."*

"Jared?" The other's reply, carried weakly on the crest of the woman's thoughts, was burdened with the perplexity of forgetfulness.

"Of course, you remember."

The Forever Man tapped inquisitively. And Jared intercepted the impression of a thin finger delving almost its entire length into a depression in the rock before producing each *tap*. Over untold generations his thumping had eroded the stone *that much!*

"I don't know you." The voice, a pained whisper, was coarse as a rock slide.

"Leah used to sort of—bring me here long ago."

"Oh, *Ethan's* little friend!" A hand that was all bone set up an audible flutter as it trembled forward. It seized Jared's wrist in a grip as tenuous as air. The Forever Man tried to smile, but the composite was grossly confused by a disheveled beard, skeletal protuberances and a misshapen, toothless mouth.

"How old *are* you?" Jared asked.

Even as he posed the question he knew it was unanswerable. Living by himself, before Leah and Ethan had come, the man would have had no life spans or gestations against which to measure time's passage.

"Too old, son. And it's been *so* lonely." The straining voice was a murmur of despair against the stark silence of the world.

"Even with Leah and Ethan?"

"They don't know what it means to have listened to loved ones pass on countless ages ago, to be banished from the beauties of the Original World, to—"

Jared started. "You *lived* in the Original World?"

"—to be cast out after hearing your grandchildren and their great-great-grandchildren grow into Survivorship."

"Did you live in the Original World?" Jared demanded.

"But you can't blame them for getting rid of a Different One who wouldn't grow old. What's that—did I live in the Original World? Yes. Up until a few generations after we lost Light."

"You mean you were there *when Light was still with man?*"

As though exhuming memories long laid to rest, the Forever Man finally replied, "Yes. I—what was it we used to say?—saw Light."

"You *saw* Light?"

The other laughed—a thin, rasping outburst cut short by a wheeze and a cough. "Saw," he babbled. "Past tense of the verb to see. See, saw, seen. Seesaw. We used to have a seesaw in the Original World, you know."

See! There was that word again—mysterious and challenging and as obscure as the legends from which it had come.

"Did you hear Light?" Jared enunciated each word.

"I saw Light. Seesaw. Up and down. Oh, what fun we had! Children scampering around with bright, shiny faces, their eyes all agleam and—"

"Did you feel Him?" Jared was shouting now. "Did you touch Him? Did you hear Him?"

"Who?"

"Light!"

"No, no, son. I *saw* it."

It? Then he, too, regarded Light as an impersonal thing! "What was it like? Tell me about it!"

The other fell silent, slumping on his ledge. Eventually he drew in a long, shuddering breath. "God! I don't know! It's been so long *I can't even remember what Light was like!*"

Jared shook him by the shoulders. "Try! Try!"

"I can't!" the old man sobbed.

"Did it have anything to do with the—eyes?"

Tap-tap-tap ...

He had returned to his thumping, burying bitter recollections and haunting thoughts under a rock pile of habit and mental detachment.

Leaving Kind Survivoress' world now was out of the question—not with the Forever Man's senile memory offering the hope of opening new passageways in Jared's search for Light. Yet, he couldn't tell Della why he had to extend their stay. So he simply pretended he was still physically unfit for immediate travel.

Apparently satisfied with this explanation for his postponement of their attempt to reach the Zivver World, Della grudgingly settled down to await his complete recovery.

That her original distrust of Leah had been an impulsive, passing thing was manifest in the subsequent lessening of tension between the two women. At one point, she even told Jared she might have been wrong in her first impression of Leah and Ethan. Why, it wasn't at all as she had initially assumed, she confessed. And Ethan, despite his handicap, wasn't the awkward, clumsy lout she had imagined him to be—not in the least.

Tactfully, Leah refrained from mind-to-mind contact with Jared and Ethan while they were in the girl's presence. To the effect that Della either forgot the woman's ability or gave it little thought.

Leah, too, had adjustments to make. Although she treated Della hospitably, Jared could always sense her misgiving over not being able to listen to the Zivver girl's mind.

These developments Jared traced with interest while he waited for the Forever Man to abandon his solitude and seek company once more. Light! What he might learn from that ageless one!

During the fifth period after their arrival, Della was splashing in the river with Ethan while Jared was sharpening his spear points on a coarse rock when Leah's thoughts came to him:

"Please *forget about the Zivver World, Jared.*"

"*You know my mind's made up.*"

"*Then you'll have to change it. The passages are full of monsters.*"

117

"How do you know? You told me you were afraid to listen to their minds."

"But I've listened to other minds—in the two Levels."

"And what did you hear?"

"Terror and panic and queer impressions I can't understand. There are monsters all over. And the people are running and hiding and creeping back to their recesses, only to flee again later on."

"Are there monsters near this world?"

"I don't think so—not yet anyway."

This posed another complication, Jared realized. Starting out for the Zivver World might not be a matter of leisure choice. It might well be that he should leave as quickly as possible.

"No, Jared. Don't go—please!"

And he detected more than selfless concern for his welfare. Lying at the base of Leah's thoughts were desperate pangs of loneliness, laced with the fear of having her simple, forlorn world cast back into the terrible solitude that had existed before he and Della arrived.

But he had made up his mind and he regretted only not having had the chance for a second talk with the Forever Man.

Just then, however, the latter's tapping came to an abrupt halt.

Jared raced across the world this time.

And, as he passed the river, Della quit splashing to ask: "Where are you running?"

"To hear the Forever Man. Afterward we'll be on our way."

Perching on the ledge, Jared asked anxiously, "Can we talk now?"

"Go away," the Forever Man groaned in protest. "You only make me remember. I don't want to remember."

"But compost! I'm hunting for Light! You can *help* me!"

Only the rasps of the other's labored breathing filled the world.

"Try to remember about Light!" Jared pleaded. "Did it have anything to do with—the eyes?"

"I—don't know. It seems I can remember something about brightness and—I can't imagine what else."

"Brightness? What's that?"

118

"Something like—a loud noise, a sharp taste, a hard punch maybe."

Jared heard the uncertainty on the Forever Man's face. Here was someone who might even tell him *what* he was searching for. But the man spoke only in riddles which were no clearer than the obscure legends themselves.

He tried to pace off his frustration in front of the nodding skeleton. Right before him might be the entire answer to how Light might benefit man, how it could touch all things at once and bring instant, inconceivably refined impressions of everything. If only the curtain of forgetfulness could be pierced!

He struck out in another direction: "What about Darkness? Do you know anything about that?"

And he heard the other shudder.

"Darkness?" the Forever Man repeated, hesitancy and sudden fear hanging on the word. "I—*oh, God!*"

"What's the matter?"

The man was trembling violently now. His wry face was a grotesque mask of terror.

Jared had never heard such fright before. The other's heartbeat had doubled and his pulse was like a wounded soubat's thrashing. Each shallow, erratic breath seemed as though it would be his last. He tried to rise, but fell back onto the ledge, burying his face in his hands.

"Oh, God! The Darkness! *The awful Darkness! Now* I remember. It's *all around* us!"

Confounded, Jared backed off.

But the recluse grabbed his wrist and, with the strength of desperation, pulled him forward. Then his anguished cries shrilled through the world and spilled out into the passageway:

"Feel it pressing in? Horrible, black, evil Darkness! Oh, God, I didn't *want* to remember! But you *made* me!"

Jared listened alertly, fearfully about him. Was the Forever Man sensing Darkness—*now?* Or was he just remembering it? But no, he had said it was "all around us," hadn't he?

Uneasily, Jared retreated and left his host fighting terror and sobbing, "Can't you feel it? Don't you see it? God, God, get me out of here!"

But Jared felt nothing except the cool touch of the air. Yet he was afraid. It was as though he had absorbed some of the Forever Man's strange fear.

Was Darkness something you felt or perhaps *seed*—rather, *saw?* But if you could *see* it, that meant you could do the same thing to Darkness that the Guardian believed could be done to Light Almighty. But—what?

For a moment Jared was desperately afraid of an indefinite menace he could neither hear, nor feel, nor smell. It was an evil, uncanny sensation—a smothering, a silence that wasn't sound-lessness at all but something both alien and akin to it at the same time.

When he reached Della she was with Leah and Ethan. Nothing was said. It was as though a bit of the incomprehensible terror had spread to all of them.

Della had already packed some food in her carrying case and Leah, resigned to his decision, had gotten his spears for him.

The silence, uncomfortable and grave, persisted as they all walked to the exit. No good-bys were offered.

A few paces down the corridor Jared turned and promised, "I'll be back." Casually letting his spears strike the wall, he sounded out the way and pushed on.

The somber world of Kind Survivoress and Little Listener and the unbelievable Forever Man slipped softly back into the immaterial depths of memory. And Jared felt a sense of poignant loss as he realized that recollections were fed by the same stuff of which dreams were made and that the only proof he would ever have of the existence of Leah's world would be in the echoes of his reflections.

CHAPTER ELEVEN

THROUGHOUT MOST OF THE TRAVEL period Della tagged silently along. That she was troubled with a restive hesitancy was evident in the worrisome expression Jared could hear on her face. Was she anxious over something he had said or done? Light knew he had already given plenty of cause for misgiving.

Since leaving Leah's world, though, he had devised an artful echo-producing system which he felt certain had escaped Della's suspicion. It consisted principally of filling the corridors with one whistled tune after another.

Eventually, the passageway pinched in on them and there was a stretch through which they had to crawl. On the other side, he rose and thudded his spear against the ground.

"Now we can breathe easier."

"Why?" She drew up beside him.

"Our rear's protected against soubats. They can't get through a tunnel that small."

She was silent momentarily. "Jared—"

Here came the question he knew she had been putting off. But he decided to forestall it. "There's a big passage up ahead."

"Yes, I ziv it. Jared, I—"

"And the air is heavy with the scent of Zivvers." He skirted a narrow chasm whose outline was carried on his reflected words.

"It is?" She pushed ahead eagerly. "Maybe we're close to their world!"

They reached the intersection and he stood there trying to determine whether they should go to the right or left. Then he tensed, instinctively gripping his spears. Mingled with the Zivver scent was a hidden, evil smell that fouled the air—an unmistakable fetor.

"Della," he whispered, "monsters have just been this way."

But she didn't hear him. Enthused, she had already stridden off along the right-hand branch of the corridor. Even now he could hear her rounding the bend a short way off.

Abruptly there was the grating sound of a rock slide, punctuated by a scream.

With the corridor's composite frozen in his memory by the shrill reflections, he raced toward the great, gaping hole that had swallowed the girl's terrified outcry.

Reaching the area of loose rock, he snapped his fingers to gain an impression of the pit's mouth. There was a solidly embedded boulder rearing up out of the rubble right next to the rim. He laid his spears down and one of them slid away, plunging over the edge and striking the wall repeatedly as it plummeted into the depth. The clatter persisted until the sound lost itself in remote silence.

Casting the other lance back onto solid ground, he frantically shouted, "Della!"

She answered in a terrified whisper, "I'm down here—on a ledge."

He thanked Light that her voice came from nearby and that there might be a chance of saving her.

Securing a grip on the boulder, he swung himself out over the chasm and snapped his fingers once more. Reflections of the sound told him she was huddled on a shelf close to the surface.

His extended hand touched hers and he gripped her wrist, lifting her out of the hole and shoving her past the area of loose rock onto firm ground.

They backed away from the pit and a final rock rolled off the incline, clattering down into the abyss. Echoes of the sharp sounds fetched the impression of the girl's calm melting away.

He let her cry for a while, then took hold of her arms and drew her erect. The sound of his breathing reflected against her face and he listened to the manner in which exposed eyes dominated her other features. He could almost feel their sharp, intense fixedness and, momentarily, he thought he might be on the verge of guessing the nature of zivving.

"It was just like what happened to my mother and father!" She nodded back toward the abyss. "It's like an omen—as if something were telling us *we* can take up where *they* left off!"

Her hands pressed down on his shoulders and, remembering the firm softness of her body against his in that other corridor, he drew her close and kissed her. The girl's response was eager at first, but quickly faded off into a perceptible coolness.

He retrieved his spear. "All right, Della. What is it?"

She wasted no time framing the question she had held back:

"What's all this about hunting for—Light? I heard you shouting at the Forever Man, asking him about Darkness too. And it scared the wits out of him."

"It's simple." He shrugged. "Like you heard me say, I'm hunting for Darkness and Light."

He sensed her perplexed frown as they started down the corridor. A manna shell thumped the side of her carrying case with each step and the sounds were sufficient to gather impressions of the passageway.

"It's not something theological," he assured. "I just have an idea Darkness and Light aren't what we think they are."

He could tell that her puzzlement had given way to mild doubt—a refusal to believe the explanation was that simple.

"But that doesn't make sense," she protested. "Everybody *knows* who Light is, what Darkness is."

"Then let's let it go at that and just say I have a different idea."

She fell silent a moment. "I don't understand."

"Don't let it bother you."

"But the Forever Man—Darkness meant something different to him. He wasn't frightened over 'evil' being all around him. He was scared of *something else,* wasn't he?"

"I suppose so."

"What?"

"I don't know."

Again she said nothing for a long while, until they had passed several branch corridors. "Jared, does all this have anything to do with going to the Zivver World?"

To a certain extent, he felt, he could be outspoken without laying his zivvership open to further suspicion. "In a way, yes. Just like zivving concerns the eyes, I believe Darkness and Light are in some way connected with the eyes too. And—"

"And you think you can find out more about them in the Zivver World?"

"That's right." He led her along a sweeping curve.

"Is that the *only* reason you're going there?"

"No. Like you, I'm also a Zivver; that's where I belong."

He heard the girl's sudden relief—the relaxation of her tenseness, the quietening of her heartbeat. His candor had evidently allayed her misgiving and now she was ready to shrug off his quest as a whim that posed no particular threat to her interests.

She eased her hand into his and they continued on around the bend. But he pulled up sharply as he caught the scent of monsters ahead. At the same time he shrank away from the left wall. For, even as he listened to its featureless surface, an indiscernible patch of silent echoes had begun playing against the moist stone.

This time he was almost prepared for the uncanny sensation. Experimentally, he closed his eyes and was instantly no longer aware of the dancing sound. He opened them again and the noiseless reflections returned immediately—like the soft touch of a shouted whisper spreading itself thin against a smooth rock surface.

"The monsters are coming!" Della warned. "I ziv their impressions—against that wall!"

He half-faced her. "You *ziv* them?"

"It's *almost* like zivving. Jared, let's get away from here!"

He only stood there concentrating on the weird, soundless noise that flowed back and forth against the wall, never reaching his ears but making his eyes feel as though someone had thrown boiling water into them. She had said she *zivved* the impressions.

Did that mean zivving was something like what was happening to him now?

Then he listened to the purely audible impressions that were coming from around the bend. There was only one monster approaching. "You go back and wait in the first side corridor."

"No, Jared. You can't—"

But he propelled her down the passage and eased into a niche in the wall. When he heard there wouldn't be enough room to draw his spear, he laid it on the ground. Then he closed his eyes, blocking off the distracting impressions the monster was hurling.

The creature had reached the bend and Jared could hear it hugging the near wall. He pressed farther into the recess.

The thing's awful, alien smell was overpowering in its nearness now. And clearly audible, too, were the numerous folds of flesh—if that's what they were—fluttering about its body. If the breathing and heartbeat were of the same intensity and frequency as the average person's, then it must be drawing even with his hiding place just about—*now.*

Lunging into the corridor, he drove his fist into what he judged to be the creature's midsection.

Air exploded from the monster's lungs as it fell forward against him. Bracing himself against what he had expected to be a slimy touch, he pounded another fist into its face.

Anxiously, he snapped his eyes open as he heard the monster collapse on the ground. He had half-expected there would be no more strange, soundless noise spreading out from the thing now that it was unconscious. And there wasn't.

Kneeling, he sent his hands out reluctantly to explore the creature. And he discovered there were no folds of flesh festooning its body. Rather, its arms, legs, torso were all covered by loosely fitting cloth of a texture even finer than the piece he had found at the entrance to the Lower Level. No wonder he had received the impression of sagging hide! Who ever heard of chestcloths or loincloths that didn't fit skintight?

His hands groped upward and encountered a duplicate of the rougher cloth he had buried in the corridor outside his world. It was drawn taut over the monster's face and held there by four ribbons tied behind its head.

He snatched the cloth away and ran his fingers over—a normal human face! It was much like a woman's or child's, smooth and completely hairless. But the cast of the features was masculine.

The monster was human!

Jared rose and his foot met a hard object. Before touching it, he bent and snapped his fingers several times. And he had no difficulty recognizing the thing. It was identical to the tubular devices left behind by the monsters in both the Upper and Lower Level.

The creature stirred and Jared dropped the object, diving for his spear.

Just then Della came sprinting down the corridor. "More monsters—coming from the other way!"

Listening around the bend, he could hear the sounds of their approach. And he was aware of the play of their mysterious mute noises along the right wall of the corridor.

He seized the girl's hand and raced on up the passage, letting his spear thump the ground so it would produce sounding impulses.

From ahead he heard the composite of a smaller branch passage. He slowed and headed cautiously into it.

"Let's go this way awhile," he suggested. "I think it'll be safer."

"Is the Zivver scent strong in this passage too?"

"No. But we'll pick it up again. These smaller tunnels usually curve back."

"Oh, well," she said, comforting herself, "at least we shouldn't be bothered by monsters for a while."

"Those aren't monsters." He surmised that, like hearing, zivving impressions weren't refined enough to distinguish between loose cloth and flesh. "They are humans."

He heard her startled expression. "But how can that be?"

"I suppose they are Different Ones—more different than all the others put together. Superior even to the Zivvers."

He let the girl lead the way and anxiously gave his attention to the enigma of the monsters. Perhaps they *were*, after all, devils.

It was commonplace to speak of the Twin Devils. But some of the lesser legends referred to, not two, but *many* demons who dwelled in Radiation. Even now he could call to mind several of them, all of whom were usually represented in personified form. There were Carbon-Fourteen; the two U's—Two Thirty-Five and Two Thirty-Eight; Plutonium of the Two Thirty-Nine Level, and that great, sulking, evil being of the Thermonuclear Depth—Hydrogen.

Of Radiation's demons there were many, now that he thought of it. And ascribed to all of them were the capacities of insidious infiltration, ingenious disguise and complete and prolonged contamination. Could it be that the devils, emerging from mythology, had finally decided to exercise their powers?

The girl slowed to pick her way over loose, uneven ground. And the noise of rocks shifting beneath their feet made it even easier to hear the way.

He found himself recalling his recent encounter with the being in the corridor. The silent sound it had cast on the wall was most remarkable, once one managed to overcome the initial horror it brought. Dwelling on those sensations, he remembered how clearly he had seemed to hear—or was it feel, or, perhaps, even ziv?—the details of the wall. He had been completely aware of each tiny ridge and crevice, each protuberance.

Then he stiffened as he drew from memory something the Guardian of the Way had said not too long ago—something about Light in Paradise touching everything and bringing to man total knowledge of all things about him. But, certainly, that material the monsters produced and hurled against the wall *couldn't* be the Almighty! And that corridor *couldn't* have been Paradise!

No. It was impossible. That meager stuff thrown so casually about the passageway by the manlike creature *hadn't* been Light. Of that he was finally and unalterably positive.

As they continued on along the rugged tunnel, his reflections turned to another matter of concern. For the moment it seemed he could almost put his finger on something that there was *less of* in this very passage! But it was too vague a concept to encourage further speculation. It must have been only wishful thinking, he decided, that was suggesting he might accidentally stumble upon Light's opposite, Darkness, in this remote, deserted corridor.

Della drew up before an opening in the wall and pulled him over beside her. "Just ziv this world!" she exclaimed buoyantly.

The wind rushing into the hole was cool against his back as he stood there listening to the delightful music of a gurgling stream and using the echoes of that sound to study other features of the medium-sized world.

"What a wonderful place!" she went on excitedly. "I can ziv five or six hot springs and at least a couple of hundred manna plants. And the banks of the river—they're *covered* with salamanders!"

As she spoke her rebounding words set up an audible composite of their surroundings. And Jared appreciatively took in several natural recesses in the left wall, a high-domed ceiling that insured good circulation, and smooth, level ground all around them.

She locked her arm in his and they walked farther into the world. The wind sweeping in from the corridor gave the air a refreshing coolness that was superior to the Lower Level's.

"I wonder if this was the world my mother was trying to reach," the girl said distantly.

"She couldn't have found a better place. I'd say it would support a large family and all its descendants for several generations."

They sat on a steep bank overhearing the river and Jared listened to the *swishing* of large fish beneath the surface while Della parceled out food from her case.

After a while he probed audibly beneath her silence and caught the suggestion of yet another area of uncertainty.

"There's something bothering you, isn't there?" he asked.

She nodded. "I still don't understand about Leah and you. I can hear now that she *did* visit you in your dreams. Yet, you yourself said she couldn't reach the mind of a Zivver."

Now he was certain she didn't know he couldn't ziv. For if she were out here for some treacherous reason, the last thing she'd do would be to let him find out she suspected him.

"I've already told you I think I'm a little different from other Zivvers," he reminded. "Right now I'm zivving a half-dozen fish in the river. You can't ziv a single one."

She lay back on the ground and, out of crossed arms, made a cushion for her head. "I hope you're not *too* different. I wouldn't want to feel—inferior."

Her words struck home with unintended mockery. And he knew that being inferior to her was what *he* had resented all along.

"If we weren't hunting for the Zivver World," she offered, yawning, "this would be a nice place to settle in, wouldn't it?"

"Maybe staying here is the best thing we could do."

He stretched out beside her and, even from the negligible echoes of his breathing, he could hear the attractive composite of the girl's face, the gentle, firm contours of her shoulders, hips, waist—all veiled in the whispering softness of near inaudibility.

"It might be a—good idea," she said drowsily, "if we—decided—"

He waited. But from her direction came only the slight body murmurs of sleep.

He turned over, crooked an arm under his head and banished the maudlin, wistful thought that had begun to obscure his purpose. He had to concede, though, that it *would* be pleasant to remain here in this remote world with Della and put out of his mind forever the Zivvers, human monsters, soubats, Upper and Lower Levels, Survivorship, and all the chains of formality and restrictions of communal law. And, yes, even his hopeless quest for Light and Darkness.

But such an arrangement was not for him. Della was a Zivver—a superior Different One. And he would always have to listen up to her and her greater abilities. It would never do. What was it he had once overheard one Zivver tell another during a raid?—"A Zivver down here is the same as a one-eared man in a world of the deaf."

That was it. He would always be like an invalid, with Della to lead him around by the hand. And in her incomprehensible world of murmuring air currents and psychic awareness of things he could never hope to hear, he would be lost and frustrated.

Even from the depths of sleep he could tell that he had lain there beside the girl a long while—perhaps the equivalent of a slumber period or more. And he surely must have been close to wakefulness when he heard the screams.

Had they been Della's, they would have jolted him from sleep. That he continued to hear them without awakening was a measure of their psychic quality. They seemed to come from deep within his mind, spawned in a vortex of projected terror.

Then he recognized Leah behind the desperate, silent outcries. He tried to distill concrete meaning from the hodge-podge of frantic impressions. But the woman was in such a panic that she couldn't put her fright into words.

Digging into the emotions of terrible astonishment and dismay, he intercepted piecemeal impressions—shouting and screaming, rushing feet and roaring bursts of silent sound that played derisively across walls which had been such a warm and real part of his childhood fantasies, an occasional *zip-hiss.*

The composite was unmistakable: The human monsters had finally found Leah's world!

"Jared! Jared! Soubats—coming in from the passage!" Della shook him awake.

He grabbed his spear and sprang to his feet. The first of the three or four beasts that had winged into the world was almost upon them. There was scarcely time to hurl Della to the ground and plant his spear in readiness for the initial impact.

The lead creature screeched down in a vicious dive and took the point of the weapon full in its chest. The lance snapped in half and the beast struck the ground with jarring impact.

The second and third hateful furies began their plunge.

He hurled the girl into the river and leaped in after her. In less than a beat the current, immensely swifter than he had estimated, was sweeping her away—toward the side wall where the stream rushed into a subterranean channel.

He heard that he couldn't overtake her in time, but he swam ahead anyway. A soubat's wingtip thrashed the water in front of him, talons barely missing their mark in a swooping attack.

At the beginning of his next stroke, his hand touched Della's hair, frothing on the surface of the water, and he secured a grip on it. But too late. The current had already sucked them into the subsurface channel and had drawn boulders of water in behind them.

CHAPTER TWELVE

SAVAGE UNDERCURRENTS FLUNG HIM TO the right and left and finally sent him plunging into the depths. He caromed against the jagged bed of the stream, then swirled upward. Jared found no air for his bursting lungs as he crashed into the submerged ceiling. Yet, he managed to maintain his grip on Della's hair.

Again and again the girl was dashed against him while he choked down the terrifying realization that the stream might rush on eternally through an infinity of rock without ever again flowing up into an air-filled world.

When he could hold his breath no longer, his head grazed a final stretch of ceiling, slipped under a ledge and bobbed to the surface. He pulled the girl up beside him and gulped great draughts of air. Sensing the nearness of the bank, he grabbed a partially exposed rock and anchored himself against it while he shoved her ashore. When he heard that she was still breathing, he crawled out and collapsed beside her.

Gestations later, after his pounding heartbeat slowed to a tolerable pace, he became aware of the roaring spatter of a nearby cataract. The noise and its distant reflections traced out the broad expanse of a high-domed world. But he started as he detected a variety of other sounds that barely pierced the audible curtain of cascading water—the remote clatter of manna shells, the thumping of rock against rock, the bleat of a sheep, voices, many voices, far and indistinct.

Confounded, he sneezed more water out of his nose. He rose, dislodging a pebble and listening to it clatter down an incline that sloped off alongside the waterfall. Then he caught a powerful, unmistakable scent and sat up, alert and excited.

"Jared!" The girl stood up beside him. *"We're in the Zivver World! Just ziv it!* It's exactly as I thought it would be!"

He listened sharply, but the composite, etched only by the dull sound of falling water, was fuzzy and confusing. Yet, he could hear the soft, fibrous tones of a manna orchard off on his left, a gaping exit to the corridor on the far right. And he picked up the impressions of many queer, evenly spaced forms in the center of the world. Arranged in rows, each was shaped like a cube with rectangular openings in its sides. And he recognized them for what they were—living quarters fashioned after those in the Original World and possibly made out of manna stalks tied together.

Della started forward, her pulse accelerating in a surge of excitement. "Isn't it a wonderful world? And ziv the Zivvers—so many of them!"

Not at all sharing the girl's enthusiasm, he followed her down the incline, gaining his perception of the terrain from echoes of the waterfall.

It was indeed a strange world. He had managed by now to garner the impressions of many Zivvers at work and play, others busy carrying soil and rocks and piling them up in the main entrance. But all that activity, without the reassuring tones of a central echo caster, gave an uncanny, forbidding cast to the world about him.

Moreover, he was sorely disappointed. He had hoped that on stepping into the Zivver domain the difference he had been hunting all his life would fairly leap out at him. Oh, it was going to be so easy! Zivvers had eyes and, in using them, they materially affected the universal Darkness, eating holes in it, so to speak—just as hearing sound ate holes in silence. And, simply by recognizing what there was less of, he was going to identify Darkness.

But he could hear *nothing* unusual. Many persons were down there zivving. Yet, everything was exactly the same here as in any other world, except for the absence of an echo caster and the presence of the sharp Zivver scent.

Della quickened her pace but he restrained her. "We don't want to startle them."

"There's nothing to worry about. We're both Zivvers."

Near enough to the settled area to intercept impressions from the rebounding sounds of communal activities, he followed the girl around the orchard and past a row of animal pens. Discovery finally came as they approached a party working on the nearest geometrical dwelling place. Jared heard an apprehensive silence fall upon the group and listened to heads twisting alertly in his direction.

"We're Zivvers," Della called out confidently. "We came here because we belong here."

The men advanced silently, spreading out to converge on them from several directions.

"Mogan!" one of them shouted. "Over here—quick!"

Several Zivvers lunged and caught Jared's arms, pinning them to his sides. Della too, he heard, was receiving the same treatment.

"We're not armed," he protested.

Others were gathering around now and he was grateful for the background of agitated voices that, in the absence of an echo caster, sounded out the more prominent details of his surroundings.

Two faces pushed close to his and he listened to eyes that were wide open and severe in their steadiness. He made certain his own lids were fully raised and unblinking.

"The *girl's* zivving," vouched someone off to his left.

An open hand fanned the air abruptly in front of his face and he was unable to keep his eyelids from flicking.

"I suppose this one is too," the owner of the hand attested. "At least, his eyes *are* open."

Jared and Della were hustled ahead between the rows of dwelling units while scores of Zivver Survivors collected from all over the world. Concentrating on vocal sounds and their reflections, he caught the impression of an immense figure pushing through the crowd and instantly recognized the man as Mogan, the Zivver leader.

"Who let them in?" Mogan demanded.

"They didn't get by the entrance," someone assured.

"They say they're Zivvers," offered another.

"Are they?" Mogan asked.

"They're both open-eyed."

The leader's voice boomed down on Jared. "What are you doing here? How did you get in?"

Della answered first. "This is where we belong."

"We were attacked by soubats beyond that far wall," Jared explained. "We jumped into the river and washed up in here."

Mogan's voice lost some of its severity. "You must have had a Radiation of a time. I'm the only one who's ever gotten in that way." Then, boastfully, "Made it through *against* the current a couple of times, too. What were you doing out there?"

"Looking for this world," Della replied. "We're both Zivvers."

"Like compost you are!" Mogan shot back. "There was only *one* original Zivver. All of us are his descendants. You're not. *You* came from one of the Levels."

"True," she admitted. "But my father was a Zivver—Nathan Bradley."

Somewhere in the background a Survivor drew in a tense breath and started forward. It was the anxious, heavy gasp of an elderly man.

"Nathan!" he exclaimed. "My son!"

But someone held him off.

"Nathan Bradley?" the man on Jared's left repeated uncertainly.

"Sure," answered another. "You heard about him. Used to spend all his time out in the passages—until he disappeared."

Then Jared felt the blast of Mogan's words directed down at him again. "What about you?"

"He's another original Zivver," Della said.

"And I'm a soubat's uncle!" the leader blurted.

Once more Jared's self-confidence slid off into doubt over the ability to carry off his disguise as a Zivver. Groping for something convincing to say, he offered, "Maybe I'm *not* an original

Zivver. You *do* have people who desert your world from time to time and who might be responsible for other spurs. There was Nathan, and there was Estel—"

"Estel!" a woman exclaimed, pushing through the crowd. "What do you know about my daughter?"

"I was the one who sent her back here the first time I zivved her out near the Main Passage."

The woman seized his arms and he could almost feel the pressure of her eyes. "Where is she? What's happened to her?"

"She came to the Lower Level listening—zivving for me. That was how everybody found out I was a Zivver. After that I couldn't very well stay down there."

"Where is my child?" the woman demanded.

Reluctantly, he related what had happened to Estel. A condoling silence fell over the world while the Survivoress was led away sobbing.

"So you swam in under the rocks," Mogan mused. "Lucky you didn't get caught in the waterfall on this side."

"Then we can stay?" Jared asked hopefully, trying to keep his eyes steady just as Mogan was doing.

"For the moment, yes."

In the silence that followed, Jared sensed a subtle change in his perception of the Zivver leader. For some reason, Mogan was unconsciously holding his breath and his heartbeat had increased slightly. Jared concentrated on the effects and detected, even more faintly, that particular physical tension which claims a person intent on some crafty purpose. Then he caught the almost inaudible impression of Mogan's hand rising slowly before him. He coughed casually and, in the reflections of the sound, discerned that the hand was slyly waiting to be clasped.

Without hesitation, his own hand shot forward and grasped the other. "Did you think I wouldn't ziv that?" he asked, laughing.

"We've got to be careful," Mogan said. "I've zivved Levelers who could hear so well that they might easily be mistaken for one of us."

"What reason would we have for coming here if we *weren't* Zivvers?"

"I don't know. But we're not taking any chances—not with those creatures stalking the passages. Even now we're sealing the entrance before they can find it. But what good would that do if they learned there was another way to get in—a way that can't be blocked?"

Mogan stepped between Jared and the girl and led them off. "We're going to keep an eye on you until we're sure we can trust you. Meanwhile, I know how you feel after swimming under those rocks. So we'll give you a chance to rest."

They were led to adjacent dwelling units—"shacks," Jared had heard one of the Zivvers call them—and were ushered in through rectangular openings. Guards were posted outside each structure.

Standing uncertainly within the enclosure, Jared cleared his throat rather loudly. Echoes of the sound brought details of a recess strikingly different from any of the residential grottoes he had known. Here, everything was an adaptation of the rectangle. There was a dining slab whose remarkably level surface was composed of husks woven tightly together and stretched across a framework of manna stalks. He laid his hand casually upon it and traced the weave. Four other stalks, he heard, served as legs to hold the level section off the floor.

He yawned as though it were a quite spontaneous expression of weariness—in case anybody should be listening or zivving—and studied the reflected auditory pattern. Arranged around the dining slab were benches of similar construction. The slumber ledge, too, was a flimsy thing supported on the apparently traditional four legs.

Then he drew up sharply, but tried not to give any indication he had discovered he was being listened to—zivved, he reminded himself. There was an elevated opening in the right wall, beyond the slumber ledge. And through that space he caught the sound of breathing purposely made shallow to insure concealment. Someone was standing out there zivving everything he did.

Very well, the safest course would be to move about as little as possible and thereby reduce the chances of betraying himself.

He yawned noisily once more, fixing in mind the position of the slumber ledge. Then he went over and lay down. They expected him to be exhausted, didn't they? Then why not *be* exhausted?

Comfortable against the softness of the manna fiber mattress, he realized that swimming the underground river *had* been an ordeal. And it wasn't too long before he was asleep.

Scream after scream crashed in on his slumber and once again he recognized the impressions as nonaudible.

Leah!

Forcing himself to remain in the dream, he tried to pry more deeply beyond the communicative link with Kind Survivoress. But the erratic contact conveyed only the essence of horror and despair. He tried to work his way physically toward the woman and succeeded in tightening somewhat the bond between them.

"Monsters! Monsters! Monsters!" she was sobbing over and over again.

And through her torment he caught the sensation of her eyelids being closed so tightly that the inner portions of her ears were roaring under the pressure; strong, determined hands gripping her arms and pulling her first this way, then that; a sharp point jabbing brutally into her shoulder; odors so frightfully offensive in their alien quality that he felt like gagging with her.

Then he intercepted the impression of fingers digging into the flesh above and below her eyes and forcing the lids open.

And instantly all Radiation screamed at him through the woman's conscious. He recognized the stentorian blare of silent sound as being identical to the stuff the monsters had hurled against the corridor walls. Only, now it was overpowering as it crashed against Leah's eyes. He feared the woman would be driven insane.

With that single convulsive sensation he lurched out of the nightmare which he knew had been no nightmare at all.

What he had heard through Kind Survivoress' eyes certainly could have been nothing but the Nuclear Fire of Radiation itself. It was as though he had crossed the boundary of material existence to share part of the torture the Atomic Demons were meting out to her beyond infinity.

Trembling, he lay motionless on the slumber ledge while the bitter aftertaste of his pseudo dream experience persisted like a fever.

Leah—gone.

Her world—empty.

The corridors—populated with monstrous humans who hurled derisive, screaming echoes that carried no sound at all. Fiendish creatures who struck their victims with paralysis before carrying them—where?

A Zivver came in, placed a shell of food on the dining surface and left without speaking. Jared went over and picked at the ration. But his interest in the meal was submerged in the remorseful realization that, during his foolhardy quest for Darkness and Light, his familiar worlds had crumbled all about him.

The pace of irrevocable change had been furious and relentless. And he grimly suspected that things would, *could* never be the same. Certainly, the malevolent beings in their outlandish attire of loosely fitting cloths had laid claim to all the worlds and passages and were now taking over with vehement determination. He was sure, too, that the design of hot-spring failures and dwindling water level was but another phase of their scheme.

And while all these things had happened he had squandered his time searching for something trivial, nursing the belief that Light was desirable. He had let the solid things of material worth slip from his grasp as he chased a whimsical breeze down an endless corridor.

Things may have been different had he, instead, organized the Levels and led the fight for Survival. There might even have been hope of returning to a normal pattern of existence, with Della as his Unification partner. Perhaps he might not even have found out she was—Different.

But it was too late now. He was a virtual prisoner in the very world which he had expected would provide the key to his futile quest for Light. And both he and the Zivvers were themselves helpless captives of the monsters who ruled the corridors.

He pushed the food aside and ran a hand through his hair. Outside, the world was animate with the audible effects of an activity period in full swing—loud conversation, children at play and, more remotely, the sound of rocks being piled on rocks as workers continued sealing off the entrance. Listlessly, he made a note of the fact that the latter noises were an excellent echo source.

But, more directly, he concerned himself with the despair which came with his conviction that he would find nothing *different* here—nothing to justify having extended his search for Darkness and Light to this world.

Among the nearer audible effects he recognized Della's voice coming from the next shack. It was a happy, excited voice that leaped from subject to subject with a bubbling rapidity and was at times obscured by the effusive words of several other women. From bits of the conversation he gathered that she had quickly located all her Zivver relatives.

The curtains parted and Mogan stood in the entrance. His bulky form, silhouetted only by back sounding, coarsely punctured the silence of the shack.

The Zivver leader beckoned with a distinctive twist of his head. "It's about time we made sure you're one of us."

Jared feigned an indifferent shrug and followed him outside.

Mogan led the way alongside a row of dwelling units as many other Zivvers fell in behind them.

They reached a clearing and the leader drew to a halt. "We're going to have a little rough-and-tumble—just you and me."

Frowning obtusely, Jared listened up at the man.

"That's the surest way to find out whether you're really zivving, don't you agree?" Mogan said, spreading his hands.

And Jared heard that they were huge hands, altogether commensurate with the size of the man. "I suppose it is," he agreed, with just a tinge of futility.

A figure broke out of the crowd and he recognized Della as she started toward him, concern heavy in the shallowness of her breathing. But someone caught her arm and drew her back.

"Ready?" Mogan asked.

Jared braced himself, "Ready."

But apparently the Zivver leader *wasn't* ready—not just yet.

"All right, Owlson," he shouted, facing the party that was still working at the entrance. "I want complete silence over there."

Then he turned to those around him. "Nobody makes a sound—understand?"

Jared concealed his hopelessness and said sarcastically, "You're forgetting I can still smell." He realized gratefully that Mogan had also forgotten about the noise of the waterfall which, thank Light, *couldn't* be silenced.

"Oh, we're not finished with the preparations," the other laughed.

Several Zivvers seized Jared's arms while another caught his hair and twisted his head back. Then wads of coarse, moist substance were stuffed into his ears and forced up his nostrils—mud!

Released into an odorless, soundless void, he brought his hands up to his face. But before he could dig the clay from his ears, Mogan closed in and locked his neck in a rocklike grip. He was wrenched off his feet and hurled violently to the ground.

Disoriented because there was no sound or scent to guide him, he sprang up and delivered a blow that landed on nothing and succeeded only in throwing him off balance again.

Dimly, he heard the laughter that filtered through the mud in his ears. But the sound was too vague to bear any impressions of Mogan's whereabouts. Fists swinging, Jared stumbled forward, circling—until the Zivver leader clouted him on the back of his neck and flattened him once more.

When he tried to rise this time, a fist pounded into his face, almost taking his head off. And he would have been convinced the following blow did accomplish that purpose if unconsciousness had not deprived him of the ability to be sure of anything.

Eventually, he responded to the stinging splash of water against his face and raised himself on an elbow. The mud had fallen from one of his ears and he could hear the circle of men who stood zivving menacingly down on him.

From within the crowd came the voices of Mogan and Della:

"Of course I knew he wasn't a Zivver," the girl was maintaining.

Irately, Mogan reminded, "And yet you brought him here."

"*He* brought *me.*" She laughed scornfully. "I couldn't have made it by myself. My only chance was to let him think I believed he was a Zivver too."

"Why didn't you tell the truth before this?"

"And give him a chance to turn on me before you could stop him? Anyway, I knew you'd find out for yourself sooner or later."

Jared shook his head dully, remembering Leah's warning against the girl and his own doubts from time to time. If he had been able to listen beyond the lobe of his ear, he might have heard that she was using him all along merely as an escort in her search for the Zivver World.

He tried to rise, but someone planted a foot on his shoulder and pressed him back against the ground.

"What's he doing here?" Mogan asked the girl.

"I don't know exactly. He's hunting for something and he thinks he might find it here."

"What?"

"Darkness."

Mogan made his way over and hauled Jared to his feet. "What did you come here for?"

Jared said nothing.

"Were you trying to find this world so you could lead a raid on it?"

When that drew no response, the leader added, "Or are you helping *the monsters* locate us?"

Still Jared offered no reply.

"We'll let you think it over awhile. You might realize a frank tongue *could* make things easier for you."

Jared, however, sensed there would be no leniency. For, as long as he was alive, they would always fear he might escape and carry out whatever purpose they suspected he was concealing.

Trussed with fiber rope, he was taken halfway across the world and shoved into a dwelling unit not far from the roaring cataract. It was a cramped shack whose wall openings were barred with stout manna stems.

CHAPTER THIRTEEN

SEVERAL TIMES DURING HIS FIRST period of confinement Jared entertained the idea of escape. Breaking out of the manna shack, he heard, would be relatively simple—if he could manage to free his hands. His wrists, however, were too securely bound.

But escape to—what? With the main entrance already blocked by the work party and the barrier it was erecting and with the savage currents of the underground river facing him in the other direction, freedom from the shack would be meaningless.

Under other circumstances, he might have eagerly listened forward to bolting captivity. But outside the Zivver domain were nothing but monster-filled corridors. Moreover, the other worlds must certainly have been laid desolate by the hateful creatures. And the only incentive that might have driven him on—the hope of finding a hidden, self-sufficient dwelling area for himself and Della—had been stripped away when the girl had turned against him.

During the second period he stood before the barred opening in the side of the shack and listened to the work crew as it finished blocking off the main entrance. Then, hopelessly, he leaned back against the wall and let the roar of the nearby cataract sweep his attention away from the other sounds.

In self-reproach he wondered what had made him think he might find Light in this miserable world. He had supposed that, since Zivvers could know what lay ahead without hearing, they must be exercising the same sort of power all men could presumably exercise in the presence of Light Almighty. And he had foolishly thought that the result of this activity would be a lessening of Darkness. But he had neglected one possibility: that lessness of Darkness might be something only the Zivvers themselves could recognize—something forever removed from his own perception as a result of sensory limitations.

Stymied in his speculations on the Light-Darkness-Zivver relationship, he went over and lay on the slumber surface. He tried to keep Della from entering his thoughts but couldn't. Then, objectively, he conceded that what she had done—tricking him into bringing her here—merely reflected a treachery basic to the nature of all Zivvers. Now Leah, on the other hand, never would have ...

Finding himself thinking of Kind Survivoress, he wondered what had happened to her. Perhaps she was even now trying to contact him from the depths of Radiation. Unless he were asleep, though, he would never know it.

For the rest of that period, except when they brought his food, he spent as much time in slumber as he could, hoping she would come again. But she didn't.

Toward the end of his third period of confinement he detected a faint noise outside the shack—a scurrying that was close enough to be audible above the throbbing spatter of the cataract. Then he caught Della's scent as she sprang forward and flattened herself against the outer wall.

"Jared!" she whispered anxiously.

"Go away."

"But I want to help you!"

"You've helped enough already."

"Use your head. Would I be free to come here now if I had acted *any other* way in front of Mogan?"

He listened to her fumbling with the solid curtain's rope lock. "I suppose you waited for the *first* opportunity to let me loose," he said disinterestedly.

"Of course. It didn't come until just now—when the Zivvers started hearing noises out in the corridor."

The last rope parted and Della entered as the rigid partition of manna stalks swung outward.

"Go on back to your Zivver friends," he grumbled.

"Light, but you're thickheaded!" She put a sawbone knife to work on his bonds. "Can you swim back through that river?"

"What difference does it make?"

"There's the Levels to return to."

His wrists fell free. "I doubt if there's enough of the Levels left to go back to, even if they *didn't* think I'm a Zivver."

"One of the secluded worlds then." And she repeated obstinately, "Can you swim the river?"

"I think so."

"All right, then—let's go." She started out of the shack.

But he held back. "You mean *you'd* go too?"

"You didn't think I'd stay here without you?"

"But this is your world! It's where you belong! Anyway, I'm not even a Zivver."

She let out an exasperated breath. "Listen—at first I was carried away with the fact that I had found someone like me. Why, I never even stopped to wonder whether it would make any difference if you *weren't* a Zivver. Then there you were lying on the ground with Mogan standing over you. And I knew it wouldn't matter if you couldn't even hear or smell or taste. *Now* can we get on our way and start hunting for that hidden world?"

Before he could say anything else, she nudged him toward the incline that would take them above the waterfall. And Jared sensed the pall of fear that lay over the Zivver World. In the distance the settled area was enveloped in a thick, ominous silence. From the indistinct echoes of cascading water, he received a composite of Zivvers drawing apprehensively back from the barricaded entrance.

Halfway up the rise he drew up sharply and his nostrils flared around a disturbing scent drifting down from above. Desperately, he scooped up several pebbles and rattled them in the hollow of his hand. In full audible clarity, Mogan stood waiting at the top of the slope.

"I suppose you think you're going to escape and tell the monsters how to get in," he said threateningly.

Jared clicked his stones rapidly, precisely, and trapped impressions of the Zivver beginning his charge downhill.

But just then the noise of a thousand cataracts abruptly rocked the world. At the same time a great, angry burst of the monsters' roaring silence stabbed into the Zivver domain from the vicinity of the blocked entrance. And, in the next beat, everyone below was screaming and scurrying frantically about as the reopened tunnel belched a mercilessly steady cone of inaudible sound.

Jared scrambled to the top of the incline, tugging Della along. Mogan, stunned, retreated with them.

"Light Almighty!" the Zivver leader swore. "What in Radiation's happening?"

"I've never zivved anything like this!" Della exclaimed, terrified.

Intense, painful sensations assaulted Jared's eyes, confusing but somehow complementing his auditory perception of the entire world. Noise reflections fetched a more or less complete impression of the fissure-rent far wall. Yet, also associated with that wall somehow were areas of concentrated silent sound that etched every detail of its surface as clearly as though he were running his hand over all of it simultaneously.

Suddenly the wall faded into relative silence and he managed to link that development with the fact that the furious cone had shifted and was at the moment cutting across another segment of the auditory composite. Now he seemed to be aware of the presence and size and shape of each shack in the center of the settlement. The fierce, screaming silence touched every object within hearing range and boiled into his conscious with agonizing ruthlessness.

He clamped his hands over his face and found immediate relief while he listened to monsters pouring in from the passageway. And with them came the familiar *zip–hisses*.

"Don't be afraid!" one of the creatures shouted.

"Throw some Light this way!" another cried.

The words reverberated in Jared's mind. What did they *mean*? Was Light actually associated with these evil beings? How could anyone *throw* Light? Once before he had wildly assumed that the stuff these creatures hurled ahead of themselves in the passages might somehow be Light. And he had at once rejected that possibility, just as he was forced to discard it anew now.

His eyes flicked open involuntarily but he only stood there, confounded by a new bewilderment. For a moment he could almost detect a deficiency of something—just as he had imagined once before that he was on the verge of putting his finger on the lessness he was seeking. Now the conviction was even firmer that there was not as much of *something* in the Zivver World as there had been before the evil beings came!

"The monsters!" Mogan shouted. "They're coming up here!"

Della screamed and the reflection of her voice brought back the impression of three of the creatures racing up the incline.

"Jared!" she tugged on his arm. "Let's get—"

Zip-hiss.

She collapsed and before he could seize her she went rolling down the incline. Frantically, Jared started after the girl. But Mogan held him back, saying, "We can't help her now."

"We can if we reach her before—"

But the Zivver leader swung him around, shoved him into the river and dived in after him.

Before Jared could shout out in protest, Mogan dragged him beneath the surface and began the desperate underwater swim against the current. He fought stubbornly against the other's grip, but the combination of giant strength and the threat of drowning swamped his struggles and there was nothing he could do but allow himself to be towed helplessly along.

At a point that he judged to be halfway through the underground stretch, the current hurled him against a boulder and whatever air he had managed to retain in his lungs escaped in an involuntary grunt. Mogan plunged for the bottom and Jared frenziedly staved off the compulsion to release his breath. His resistance snapped finally and a great mouthful of water boiled down his windpipe.

147

He revived to the rhythmic motion of the Zivver's broad hands as they pressed down on the small of his back and withdrew, pressed and withdrew. He retched and coughed up warm water.

Mogan stopped pumping air into his lungs and helped him to a sitting position. "Guess I was wrong about you plotting with those creatures," he said apologetically.

"Della!" Jared exclaimed between coughs. "I've got to get back in there!"

"It's too late. The place is filled with monsters."

Jared listened anxiously for the river. But he heard no water anywhere around them. "Where are we?" he demanded.

"Out in a lesser passage. After I dragged you ashore I had to haul you off before the soubats got us."

Listening to reflections of the words, Jared traced out the details of a tunnel that broadened ahead after issuing from the constriction of pinched walls behind them. And from back there came the infuriated sounds of the soubats that couldn't get through.

"We're not headed toward the main corridor, are we?" he asked disappointedly.

"The opposite direction. It beats fighting off soubats bare-handed."

Jared rose and steadied himself against the wall. There might have been a chance of overtaking the monsters in the larger passageway, but the soubats had overruled that possibility, he conceded glumly. "Where does this tunnel lead?"

"Never been this way before."

Realizing he had no choice, Jared followed the reflections of their voices down the corridor.

Later, when he stumbled for a second time, he wondered why he was groping around in a noiseless passage without sounding stones. He felt along the ground until he found a pair of pebbles that almost matched, then filled the air with *clicks* before continuing.

After a while Mogan said, "You hear pretty good with those things, don't you?"

"I manage." Then Jared heard he was being abrupt for no reason at all, unless it was because he resented the Zivver's having kept him from trying to reach Della—an attempt which certainly would have failed anyway.

"I've had practice with the things," he added more affably.

"I suppose they're all right for someone who can't ziv," Mogan ventured, "but I'm afraid the noise would drive me crazy."

They traveled in silence for some time. And, as Jared's steps took him farther from the Zivver domain, the possibility that he might never hear Della again burdened him with despair. He knew finally that he would have settled with her in a secluded world and that it would have made no difference whether she was his superior or not—as long as they could be together.

But now she was gone and another—the most vital—part of his universe had crumbled beneath him. He berated himself for having failed to recognize what she meant to him, for his distorted sense of values that prompted him to attach more importance to an insane quest for Light and Darkness. Finding her, he vowed, would be his single purpose, even if it carried him to the Thermonuclear Depths of Radiation. And if he couldn't snatch her back from the monsters, then Radiation would be his deserved punishment.

They passed a lesser chasm and the Zivver leader fell in alongside him. "Della said you were hunting for Light and Darkness."

"Forget it," Jared snapped, determined to forget it himself.

"But I'm interested. If you had been a Zivver, I was going to have a talk with you."

Somewhat curious, Jared asked, "About what?"

"I don't put any stock in the legends either. I always thought the Great Light Almighty was unnecessary glorification for something commonplace."

"You did?"

"I've even decided what Light *is*."

Jared halted the march. "What is it?"

"Warmth."

"How do you figure that?"

"There's warmth all around us, isn't there? Greater warmth we call 'heat'; lesser warmth, 'cold.' The warmer a thing is, the more impressions it sends to a Zivver's eyes."

Jared nodded pensively. "And it lets you know about things without feeling, hearing, or smelling them."

Mogan shrugged. "Which is what the legends say Light does."

There was something inconsistent here, but Jared couldn't quite decide what. Perhaps it was just his reluctance to admit Light might be something as prosaic as heat. He resumed the march and stepped more briskly as he heard a larger corridor ahead.

At the same time Mogan said, "I ziv another passage up there, a big one."

Jared trotted forward, sounding his clickstones more rapidly to accommodate the greater speed. But he jolted to a stop as he broke into the larger tunnel.

"What's wrong?" Mogan paused beside him.

"This place reeks with the scent of monsters!" Jared flared his nostrils, sucking in samples of air. "That's not all. There's the smell of Upper and Lower Level people too—almost as strong as the other odor."

From his clickstone echoes he received an impression of the Zivver leader running a hand over his brow.

"This corridor's Radiation on the eyes!" Mogan exclaimed. "Too much warmth. It's hard to ziv one thing from another."

Jared, too, had felt the heat. But he was concerned with a different consideration. There was something familiar about this stretch of passage, about its formations of tumbled rocks. Then it struck him. Of course—they were just outside the Original World! He clicked his stones again and detected the slab behind which he and Owen had hidden from his first encounter with a monster. Around the bend to his right would be the Original World entrance and, beyond that, the Barrier and the Levels.

"Which way should we go?" Mogan asked.

"To the left," Jared suggested impulsively, shoving off.

After a few paces, he said, "So you think heat is Light."

"I do."

"And Darkness?"

"Simple. Darkness is coolness."

Now Jared had his finger on the inconsistency. "You're wrong. Only Zivvers can sense heat and cold from a distance. Tell me one legend that holds Light will be the exclusive property of Zivvers. All the beliefs say *everybody* will be Reunited with Light."

"I've got that figured out too. It's just that the Zivvers are the first step toward general Reunion."

Jared was going to protest that assumption also. But he had just negotiated a bend in the corridor and now he drew back reflexively. Riding the crest of his clickstone echoes were the details of another curve ahead. And he was profoundly aware of a tremendous flow of silent sound pouring from around that bend. It was as though a thousand human-inhuman creatures were marching in his direction, all hurling screaming silence before them.

"I can't ziv a thing!" Mogan complained desperately.

Jared listened but heard no audible sounds of monsters around the bend. Cautiously, he pressed forward, determined this time to keep his eyes open. His face contorted in protest to volition and muscles grew taut as they tried unsuccessfully to close the lids they controlled. Squinting and trembling, he found himself going ahead and forgetting to use his stones.

Mogan came along, trailing by a considerable distance, though, and emitting an occasional distressed oath.

Jared reached the bend and plunged swiftly around it, afraid that if he hesitated he might turn and flee. Now the dreadful stuff was flowing into his eyes with the force of a hundred hot springs and he could no longer keep them open. Tears streaming down his cheeks, he stumbled forward, relying once more on his pebbles.

His steps, however, were mired in terror. For, from ahead came *no* echoes of his *clicks—none at all!* But that was impossible! Never had anyone heard a noise that didn't reflect from *all* directions. Yet, here was a great, incredible gap in a sound pattern!

His fear finally became an absolute barrier and he could go no farther. Standing as motionless as though he had been planted there like a manna tree, he shouted.

There were *no* reflections of his voice from ahead, from above, from either side! From behind, the returning sound etched the presence of a great wall of rock that towered many times the height of even the Zivver World dome. And in this wall he detected the muffled hollowness of the corridor he had just left.

The decision struck him with the force of a falling boulder: *He was in infinity!* And it was not an endless stretch of rock that surrounded him, but an unbounded expanse of—*air!*

Terrified, he backed toward the passage. For all beliefs had held that there were only two infinities—Paradise and Radiation.

Another step and he collided with Mogan.

The Zivver leader exclaimed, "I can't even keep my eyes open! Where are we?"

"I—" Jared choked on his words. "I think we're in Radiation."

"Light! I smell it!"

"The smell of the monsters. But it's not *their* scent at all—just the odor of this place."

Dismayed, Jared retreated again toward the passageway. Then he became more aware of the intense heat and readily understood why the other's zivving ability had been deafened. Mogan was used to the normal range of warmth in the worlds and corridors. Here, the heat of all the boiling springs in existence was pouring down from above.

And, abruptly, Jared knew he could not leave this infinity without definitely identifying it. Already he suspected which one it was. The heat was a more than sufficient clue. But he had to make certain. Bracing himself against the expected pain, he opened his eyes and let the tears out.

The uncanny impressions that assailed him were fuzzy this time and he wiped his cheeks with the back of his hand.

Then the composites came—sensations that he suspected were something like ziv impressions. He was uncannily aware—through the medium of his eyes themselves—that the ground sloped away in front of him toward a patch of tiny, slender things that swayed this way and that in the distance. Vaguely, he was reminded of manna trees. Only, their tops were lacy and delicate. And he remembered the Paradise plant legend.

But *this* was an infinity of *heat*, not at all suggestive of heavenly things.

Between the trees he zivved the details of small, geometrical forms, arranged in rows like the shacks in the Original World. Another supposed feature of Paradise.

But *monsters* dwelled here.

Suddenly he directed his attention to one paramount fact:

He was receiving detailed impressions of an infinite number of things at one time, without having to hear or smell them!

Which was a capability possible only in the presence of the Great Light Almighty.

This, then, was it.

This was the end of his search.

He had found Light. And Light *was*, after all, the stuff the monsters hurled ahead of themselves in the passageways.

But Light was not in Paradise.

It was in the infinity of Radiation with the Nuclear monsters.

All the legends, all the tenets were bitterly misleading.

For man there was *no* Paradise.

And, with the Atomic Demons roaming the passageways at will, humanity had reached the end of its material existence.

He threw his head back in desperation and full against his face crashed the deadliest silent sound imaginable.

It was an impression so fierce that it seemed to boil his eyes right out of their sockets.

Screaming at him in all its fury was a great, round vicious thing that dominated Radiation with incredible force and heat and malignant majesty.

Hydrogen Himself!

Jared spun around and bolted for the passage, hardly aware that he had, at the same time, heard a noise on the incline before him.

Mogan shouted. But the anguished outcry was interrupted by a *zip-hiss*.

Jared made it back into the corridor, racing frantically after the echoes of his clickstones.

CHAPTER FOURTEEN

HARDLY AWARE MOGAN WAS NO longer with him, Jared welcomed the intimate security of the Passageway's walls as they closed in about him once more. The *zip-hiss* that had accounted for the Zivver leader's absence was only an insignificant memory against his greater dismay.

Stumbling, he pushed on toward the first bend. His eyes, boiling and dripping tears of protest, were still feeling the awful pressure of the monster stuff that had crammed all the empty space in that horrible infinity of Radiation.

He collided with a boulder, fell, picked himself up and raced on around the curve, only dimly aware that he was making his way among the hazards without the benefit of audible impulses.

Eventually he drew up and clung uncertainly to a slender hanging stone, waiting for his breathing to come under control.

Everything was clear now, ironically clear. All that stuff in infinity was—Light. It was the same Light he had spent a lifetime seeking. Only, it had turned out to be an evil thing because it was part of Radiation itself.

Then suddenly he felt the impact of yet another incredible realization:

Now he knew what Darkness was too!

It was here—in this very corridor—in all the corridors he had ever known, all the worlds he had ever visited. In his entire lifetime he had never been out of the Darkness, except for those few occasions on which he had encountered the monsters. There had been no way of recognizing it until he had first experienced Light.

But it was so simple now.

The infinity behind him was filled with Light. In the corridor ahead was a decided lessness of the stuff. And around the next curve, there would be an absolute absence of Light, a totality of Darkness—so complete, so universal that he might have lived in it for ten thousand gestations without ever knowing it was there.

Reeling under the perplexing weight of strange, new concepts, he continued down the corridor, hands extended uncertainly. And, through the medium of his eyes alone, he could fully sense the Lightlessness that loomed ahead, stark as the most profound silence he had ever known—a heavy, thick curtain of Darkness.

With hesitant steps, he negotiated the bend and edged into the immaterial barrier, flinching as the Darkness closed inexorably in about him. Now, in feeling his way forward, his hands maintained a steady, probing motion. And, humiliated, he was reminded of how his less sensitive brother Romel had to grope his way into a dense silence.

With his next step his foot fell off into the emptiness of a shallow depression and he pitched forward clumsily. Before rising he gathered up a pair of pebbles and rattled them in his hand.

But now the *clicks* seemed remote and alien. Only with great concentration could he define from the echoes the impressions of what lay ahead. And he wondered whether faulty hearing might be one of the immediate effects of Radiation sickness. Then he felt a fear as intense as the Darkness around him when he recalled another legend: Anyone who encountered Radiation could expect all kinds of severe illnesses—fever, deafness, fatal vomiting, shedding of the hair and blindness, whatever that was.

Yet, physical self-concern was buried under a bitterness that engulfed him like the stifling vapor of a boiling pit. Ahead stretched only a future as empty of material things as the vast infinity from which he had just escaped.

His every purpose was now nothing more than a shattered dream—his worlds decimated; Della gone; his search for Light ended in the agonizing remorse of disappointment and delusion.

All his life he had chased a ringing hope down an intriguing corridor, only to overtake it finally and find that it was no more than a wisp of air.

Plodding on into the Darkness, he rattled his pebbles desperately, paying the price of severe attention for each impression he wrung from the no longer familiar echoes. In a frenzy, he wrested as much perceptive content as he could out of each reflected tone. And even then he had to pause occasionally and send a hand fumbling ahead to touch out an indistinct obstacle.

He reached the intersecting passage through which he and Mogan had arrived at this larger corridor and, a few steps farther, the reflections of his *clicks* began gathering impressions of the Original World's resonant hollowness off to his left.

Then he clamped his fist around the rattling stones and snuffed out their noises. Tensing, he backed off before the sounds that were coming from ahead— direct sounds he should have heard many beats earlier.

Voices—many of them. The corridor was loud with monsters! He could even pick up their scent. And mingled with it was the characteristic odor of Zivvers—unconscious captives, no doubt, who were being borne by the demons.

He retreated from the center of the passage and crouched between two outcroppings, making certain he was in an echo void. It occurred to him, however, that if he wanted to conceal himself from the creatures, he would have to make sure he was in a Light void too. So he backed even farther into the recess.

Now he was becoming aware of the Light that was beginning to seep into the fissure. But, determined to have nothing further to do with the monster stuff which had already begun to rob him of his hearing, he closed his eyes tightly.

With the auditory composite of the monsters and Zivvers firmly in mind, he turned his attention to the conversation between a pair of demons passing by:

"... glad we decided to finish up with the Zivvers."

"So am I. They're not too hard to bring around, since they already know how to use their eyes."

"They indoctrinate easy. Now you take that last group from the Upper ..."

That conversation was superseded by another as two more monsters filed by:

"... damned intriguing, this zivving phenomenon. Thorndyke says he wants to study it closely."

"It's not all *that* peculiar. Once Radiation stimulates genetic change, you can expect any kind of mutation, including vision in the infrared range, I suppose."

Many of the words were meaningless. Nor could Jared remember the name "Thorndyke" listed among the hierarchy of Nuclear demons.

The last of the procession passed and he only crouched there, lost in disappointment. He had listened intensely and sniffed avidly. But there had been no trace of Della among the captives.

He had almost decided to continue on toward the Lower Level when he heard yet another demon coming from the direction of the Barrier, however. And he almost bolted from concealment as he caught the scent of Della at the same time.

Keeping his eyes firmly closed so there would be no distraction from the Light impressions, he waited tensely. Finally the creature drew abreast of the fissure and Jared hurled himself upon it, driving his shoulder into its ribs.

Della's inert weight came down upon him, but he shook free and lunged after her captor. He managed to catch the thing's throat in the bend of his arm, but decided against wasting the time it would take to throttle the life out of it. Instead he pounded his fist against the creature's jaw until it went limp.

Lifting the girl onto his shoulder, he snapped his fingers to sound out his bearings, then raced on into the temporary security of the Original World. As best he could, he interpreted the reflections of the *snaps* and made his way across the central clearing. At random, he selected one of the shacks for further concealment.

Inside, he deposited Della on the floor and sat just within the opening, alertly listening for suspicious sounds.

Hundreds of breaths passed before he sensed the girl's return to consciousness and heard her draw in an erratic breath. He hurried over and clamped a hand across her mouth in time to block a scream.

Against her terrified struggling he whispered, "It's Jared. We're in the Original World."

When the fright had drained away he released her and told her what had happened.

"Oh, Jared!" she exclaimed after he had finished. "Let's go find our hidden world while we still have the chance!"

"As soon as we can be sure there aren't any more demons out in the corridors."

Wearily, she rested her head against his arm. "We'll find a pleasant world, won't we?"

"The best. If it isn't just like we want it, we'll build it over to suit ourselves."

"We'll carve out a grotto first and then—" She hesitated. "Listen! What's that?"

At first he heard nothing. Then, as their attentive silence deepened, there came a faint *thump-thump, thump-thump*. It was as though rocks, or something even harder, were striking one another. But, at the moment, he was more concerned over the fact that Della had heard it first. Could his encounter with Radiation have produced *that* degree of deafness already? Or was it merely that he was confused by the memory of having gained impressions through Light impulses and was forgetting how to use his ears?

"What is it?" she asked, rising.

"I don't know." He groped his way out of the residential structure. "It seems to be coming from this next shack."

Homing in on the sound, he followed it through the entrance of that other living unit and stood listening to it flow up from a square opening in the floor. Della clung to his hand and he felt her start as she zivved the presence of the artificial pit.

He moved closer and listened sharply into the hole that descended at an acute angle instead of boring straight down. Now he could hear the *thump-thump* being distinctly modulated by an

159

abrupt, regular series of elevations that stretched along the entire lower surface of the slanting tunnel.

"There are steps going down as far as I can hear," he said.

"To where?"

He shrugged inadequately.

"Jared, I'm frightened."

But he was rigid with thought, one foot poised above the first step. "The legends say Paradise isn't far from the Original World."

"There's no Paradise down there! If we're going to go *anywhere*, let's get on with the search for our own world."

He took the first step, reached for the next. He had found, to his distress, that *Radiation* was close to the Original World. But that didn't mean Paradise, too, wasn't *somewhere* around here.

Moreover, his attention was so firmly attached to the *thump-thump, thump-thump* that he had no incentive to consider anything else. It was a peculiar, enchanting sound that drew him down, down.

Thump-thump-throb, thump-thump-throb ...

The *clacks* were crude, yet delicate. They were sharp and precise, profoundly clear. It was as though a super echo caster were sounding far in the distance—a caster whose reflections were so perfect that there wasn't a detail of setting they couldn't wring out of one's surroundings.

Even with his hearing so dulled by having experienced the vast infinity of the Nuclear devils, he could discern features of the stones around him that he would never have been able to detect otherwise. Each crack and niche in every step, each fissure in the walls, all the minute rises or depressions of the surfaces— *everything* was clearly audible. Why, the sonic composites he was receiving now were almost as perfect as those weird ones which had come in through his eyes when all the Light in Radiation had engulfed him!

Impotent before the allurement of that marvelous caster, he hastened his descent. It was like approaching the most perfect artificial echo producer ever devised. Such a caster could, of course, exist only in Paradise.

Thump-throb, clank-chunk .... *Thump-throb, clank-chunk, spat* ...

His ears opened in fascination to the subtle counterpoints that swam closer to the surface of the dominant sound as he neared its origin. The volume of the whole swelled about him like a soft embrace. The perfection and precision of these tones were incredible.

Thump-throb, ping-spatss ...

The bold, bass tones sounded out the exact pattern of every major prominence about him. Even without attentive listening he could keep track of each insignificant motion of Della's arms and legs as she trod the steps. And the finer, more highly pitched notes filled in the composite to a degree of completion that was exquisite. Take that delicate *pinkle-twang*—it required no concentration at all to listen to each strand of hair that comprised the girl's banded tress which now hung casually over her shoulder.

Thump-throb, ping-spat, chunk, tut-tut-tut-tut ...

He tuned his ear to the minor stuttering vibration. Listening to its unbelievably distinct tones, he heard even the imperceptible creases of flesh that comprised the girl's frown. The impressions that came from her long eyelashes were as clear as though he had scores of tiny fingers feeling each one individually.

He began taking the steps two at a time, fearing for a while that, in racing toward the infinite sonic beauty of Paradise, he might also be descending an infinitely long flight of stairs. But, then, the steps curved to the right and at last he could hear the opening at the bottom of the pit, not too far ahead.

"Let's turn around!" Della pleaded, huffing. "We'll *never* get back up all these steps!"

But he only went faster. "Don't you hear this might be what I've been searching for all along? I wasn't trying to find *Light*. I was really hunting for Paradise, but I didn't realize that until now."

He reached the bottom of the stairs and drew the girl to a halt beside him. They stood under a broad arch of stone that opened up on a vast enclosure, many times more expansive than even the spacious Zivver domain. Enraptured, he swayed before the rich, tremolant sound and let the mighty avalanche of ideal tones pour down upon him. It was easily the most entrancing experience of his life. He had found an auditory beauty beyond imagination. And such unbounded excellence of concord and rhythm transported him with delight, filled him with intense emotions of gratification, self-assurance.

Constraining his exuberant reaction, he listened to the world that stretched before him.

A Paradise that was practically—*all water?*

Impossible! Yet, there it was—one vast, level expanse that modified the reflecting tones with nothing but liquid fluidity.

He heard now that he was standing on a ledge only slightly higher than the surface of the water. And there was no other dry ground his ears could detect. From the far end of the world came the profound roar of an immense cataract that poured out of the ceiling.

The ledge extended but a few paces to his right. On his left it followed the natural curvature of the wall and he traced its audible details around to the very origin of the perfect-sounding tones.

Paradise's echo caster was a cluster of tremendous cubic structures. Each was many times the size of even the largest shack in the Original World. And they were smothered in a complicated pattern of huge tubes that stretched up out of the water, coiling and intertwining, and disappeared into the sides of the structures.

From the tops of the super shacks reared hundreds of tubes that shot straight up and bored into the ceiling in many directions.

Confounded, he studied the *thump-throb, tut-tut-tut-tut* that was bringing all these details to his ears.

"What *is* this place?" Della whispered apprehensively. "Why is there so much heat?"

Now that she had mentioned it, he *was* aware of the clinging warmth. And it all seemed to be coming from the huge shacks that were producing the ideal-sounding echoes. Somehow he had begun to doubt seriously that he was in Paradise.

"What do you ziv, Della?" But even as he asked the question, he sensed that her eyes were closed.

"I'm not zivving—not with all this heat. It's too much." She seemed frightened and confused.

"Try it."

She hesitated a long while before he caught the impression of her eyes flicking open.

But she only gasped and threw her hands in front of her face. "I can't! It's too painful!"

Then he realized that, all the while, his *own* eyes hadn't been open. He raised his lids and *saw* (that would be the proper word for it, he remembered) nothing.

"Didn't you ziv anything at all?" he asked.

Stubbornly, she continued shielding her face. "Some shacks—enormous ones. And a lot of stems reaching up from the water. Everything after that was too hot. I couldn't keep my eyes on it."

Impulsively, he swung his head back in the direction of the shacks. There was Light over there now! Not the kind he had experienced in infinity, but the kind the monsters carried—two cones darting here and there among the noise-making structures.

Puzzled over his silence, the girl asked, "What is it?"

"Monsters!"

Then he heard one of the creatures shouting to the other above the clamor of the multiple echo caster:

"Did you dampen the fourth reactor?"

"I shut it down completely. That takes care of the last few springs in the Upper Level, according to the diagram."

"How about those scattered springs—the ones fed by the second reactor?"

"Thorndyke says to let them go on flowing. If we miss anybody, they'll have a place to stay until we can find them."

Heartsick, Jared retreated toward the stairs. He had been right all along. The monsters *were* responsible for the boiling-pit failures. And now he heard how precarious had been the position of the Survivors through all the generations. At any chosen moment the demons could have deprived them of their principal means of existence!

Abruptly the cone of light swung in his direction. He turned and bolted for the stairs, prodding Della ahead of him.

"They're coming!" he warned.

At full speed they bounded upward. There was a moment, after he had climbed hundreds of steps, that he considered slowing the pace so they could catch their breath. But he realized just then that he was also receiving faint Light composites of the things around him. Which meant the monsters were already on their way up!

His lungs boiling in protest, he put on a burst of speed nevertheless and dragged the girl along. Desperately, he wondered how far they were from the top.

"I—I can't go on!" she complained.

When she collapsed, the sudden resistance of her weight against his grip almost pulled him off balance. He helped her up and, with an arm around her waist, resumed his dash up the stairs.

Despite his help, she fell again and, when he tried to lift her, he dropped beside the girl. He would have lain there forever. But this was their last chance; if they failed now, there would never be a secure, secluded world for them.

He struggled erect, cradled the girl in his arms and forced his numb legs back into motion. Each step sent a new throb of pain through his side. Each frantically gulped lungful of air seemed as if it would be his last.

Then, finally, he heard the opening above and drew a scant measure of encouragement from the nearness of his goal. Only vaguely did he wonder, however, where he would muster the strength to find concealment after they reached the Original World.

An eternity later he hauled himself and the girl up over the last step and crawled onto the floor of the shack. He gave Della a shove forward. "Hide in one of the other units—quick!"

She dragged herself ahead, staggering on through the entrance. Outside, she pitched forward and he heard only the violent rasping of her breath as she lay there motionless.

He managed to pull himself erect. But paralyzing exhaustion sent him reeling against an inner wall. He collided with a bulky object and his auditory impressions of the shack spun dizzily about him. He crashed into something else and collapsed, retaining his consciousness not even long enough to feel the impact of all the furnishings that tumbled down on top of him.

CHAPTER FIFTEEN

"DON'T LIE THERE, JARED! GET up and save yourself!"

Distorted with anxiety, Leah's thoughts spanned the distance from Radiation. And Jared was vaguely disturbed by the fact that he couldn't even recall having entered a dream.

"The demons—they're coming up the steps!"

He stirred against the pressure of all the things which, he remembered now, had tumbled down upon him in the shack. But somehow he couldn't quite pull himself back to consciousness.

"I can't talk and keep track of the monsters at the same time!" Leah went on frantically. *"They don't know you're there, but they heard all that noise. They'll find you and bring you back to Radiation!"*

He was perplexed over his passive reaction to the warning. His stupor, he reasoned, must be the result of more than mere exhaustion.

Through the medium of Leah's conscious, he strove for a composite of the physical things around her. And he sensed, from the audible impressions stored in her mind, that she lay on a slumber surface she had learned to call a "bed." She was in some sort of a shack that was closed off by a rigid curtain (the unfamiliar word "door" was suggested). Her arms were bound to the sides of the bed. And her eyes were stubbornly closed because she knew that if she opened them they would be assailed by the incomprehensible stuff she had been told was "light." It was seeping in around the edges of a flexible curtain that hung in front of the—"window."

Then he caught a surge of pure terror as he heard the door of her grotto—"room," rather—opening. And he listened in on an auditory impression of two of the human-inhuman creatures entering.

"How's our telepath today?" he heard one of them ask.

"We're going to spend a little time with our eyes open, aren't we?" the other added.

Jared sensed the awful fright lapping at Leah's self-control as she cringed from the creatures.

As though the experience were his own, he felt her arm being seized in a firm grip. Then a sharp pain erupted in the flesh above the right elbow. At the same time, he intercepted the psychic and sonic counterparts of her scream.

"There," said one of the monsters. "That'll help keep you from coming down with something."

From somewhere in Jared's material background came a distant *zip-hiss*. But he was too absorbed in what was happening to Kind Survivoress to give it more than superficial attention.

It had been periods now since the monsters had seized Leah. And he could only wonder what inconceivable torture they had put her through.

"How's she doing?" asked the nearer creature, taking her wrist in a gentle grip between thumb and forefinger.

"We're having a rough time bringing her around. Seems to be immune to facts and logic."

"We'll just have to stick with it. Thorndyke says there was another telepath in our own complex two or three generations back. She was pretty sensitive too, but she didn't have to put up with what this one's going through."

Jared felt a hand come to rest on Leah's forehead and heard one of the creatures say, "All right, now—let's open our eyes."

At that instant the strand of communicative contact snapped as unrestrained fear choked the woman.

Jared pushed a stone bench off his chest and sat up, feeling his head. There was a clot of blood embedded in his hair and, above it, a swelling of lacerated scalp.

He cast off more of the shack's furnishings and rose. Although he snapped his fingers intently, he received but indistinct composites of the objects that had pinned him down, of the square pit which lay between him and the entrance.

Then, recalling the *zip-hiss* he had heard while in contact with Leah, he bolted outside.

There was no audible trace of Della's breathing or heartbeat. He banged his fist against the side of the shack and wrung impressions out of the returning echoes. The ground in front of him was utterly bare.

Eventually he caught the scent, several hundred beats old, of the monsters that had passed. He knelt and swept the ground with his hands, exploring the spot where the girl had collapsed. The soft dust clearly bore the imprint of her body. But she had lain there so long ago that the surface had already given up the warmth it had captured from her.

Stunned, he trudged toward the Original World entrance. Della was gone—recaptured by the monsters who must have assumed she was the one who had made all the noise in the shack. And they had reclaimed her so long ago that now there was no hope of overtaking them before they reached Radiation.

What a bungling fool he was! As though his fortune had been graced by some power greater than Light, he had received a second chance even after having lost Della the first time. Against inconceivable odds, he had wrested her from her captors. But, instead of fleeing to remote seclusion, he had dawdled in the meaningless depths below this world—until the demons had gotten another opportunity to carry her off.

Bitter with self-reproach and bowed by an oppressive sense of futility, he paused in the corridor outside the Original World. The silence that extended toward Radiation was as thick as any he had ever heard. He tried not to think of the torment Leah was being subjected to, of the possibility that by now Della herself might be undergoing the same brutal indignities.

He took an uncertain step in that direction, then checked himself and listened helplessly down at his empty hands. Without weapons he could do nothing against the vicious forces of infinity.

But he *could* arm himself! If the Lower Level was as desolate as he had been led to believe, then he would probably meet little opposition on returning there. Possibly no one left in that world would even remember he was supposed to be a Zivver.

He gathered up a pair of stones and rattled them vigorously as he stepped off toward the Barrier and the worlds beyond. Now that he had finally committed himself to invading Radiation, he was surprised to find that the challenge did not, at the moment, impress him as being all that horrifying.

Click–click–click–click ...

The echoes rebounding from the walls and obstacles of the passageway were bare and featureless and a growing uncertainty slowed his pace. He could scarcely hear the details of the things about him!

Anxiously, he cupped a hand behind an ear. When that did no good, he extended the hand in front of him where its groping could supplement the inadequate auditory impressions.

He had practically no listening ability left at all! The memory of having received eye-stimulating composites in Radiation was so strong and vivid that he could barely hear the present sonic ones.

His next step sent his shin crashing against a minor outcropping and he went hobbling forward as he swore at his own clumsiness and deafness. He collided with a hanging stone, lost his balance and fell on the edge of a yawning pit.

Confounded, he picked himself up and went ahead even more slowly, shuffling each foot forward before putting his full weight on it.

He fought down a growing fear of the unhearable hazards, staying within arm's reach of the right wall. And he listened suspiciously as he neared the area of the Barrier. He sensed more than heard that there was something out of place. He recognized what it was when he arrived at the spot where the obstruction of piled stones should have been. There he found nothing. The Nuclear demons had even destroyed the shield which protected the worlds from the evils of infinity. They had torn it down in order to remove the Survivors and animals. Faintly, he could smell the lingering scent of the latter in the corridor.

Tossing away his pebbles, he found two large rocks and clapped them resoundingly together again and again. But the reflections of even those vigorous *clacks* returned practically unmodified, bearing only the meagerest of impressions.

With the next frantic clap, the rocks crumbled in his fists, leaving him clutching only handfuls of dirt. Despondently, he unclenched his fingers and let the particles trickle from his grip. Light! But he couldn't even hear the impact of the powder on the ground, much less the sound of its falling!

Frightened over his mounting incapacity, he floundered on. A few steps later he came up sharply against the right wall of the corridor and rebounded against a jagged stone formation, taking skin off his elbow.

Then he realized he was once more in the presence of Light.

The patch of silent sound clung to a rock up ahead, just as that other blotch of Light had covered the wall outside the Upper Level. Almost noiseless in volume, it filled the corridor with soft warmth.

Jared went ahead a bit more certainly, letting his eyes intercept the uncanny impressions of stone formations and hazards that were within range of the monster stuff.

The more cautious side of his judgment cried out a warning against using those unhearable composites to pick his way past the obstacles. But his hearing had already been so dulled by exposure to Radiation that, surely, this weak Light could increase the deafening effect but little.

He negotiated that stretch of passageway without faltering, even though he hadn't used his ears at all. When he turned the next bend, however, he pulled back against a sudden apprehension.

Now there was no more Light touching him. It was as though he were smothering in the great, silent folds of that clinging curtain of Darkness. He could feel it pressing in on him with a force that was strange, ominous, heavy.

He wanted to scream and charge deafly ahead, hoping that when he reached the familiar setting of the Lower Level he would no longer be tormented by this awful fear.

Then he remembered the Forever Man and how that pathetic recluse had cringed in stark terror from something which at the time had been meaningless, as far as Jared was concerned.

But it was different now. Now he *knew* what Darkness was. And he could fully appreciate the Forever Man's unreasoning fright. Rigid with dismay, he listened intensely all around him. With his hearing and smell practically gone, Light only knew *what* might be lurking in the flexures of that impenetrable curtain—waiting to spring upon him!

His ears finally *did* manage to intercept a distant sound and he shied away from it. But before he could turn and bolt off, the direct auditory impressions resolved themselves into words:

"Light be thanked—the Period of Reunion has arrived."

He recognized Philar, the Guardian of the Way.

And a handful of voices answered, "Thank Light."

Philar: "Darkness will be swept away before Survivor."

Voices: "And Light will prevail."

It was almost a chant. But the expressions lacked the sincerity of forceful conviction.

Jared went forward to meet the party.

Philar: "We will open our eyes and feel the Great Light Almighty."

Voices: "And there will be no more darkness."

"Go back!" Jared shouted. "Don't come this way!"

The party halted as he reached them in the Darkness.

"Who's that?" demanded the Guardian.

"Jared. You can't—"

"Out of the way. We are told Reunion is at hand."

"Who told you that?"

"Light's Emissaries. They said we must all come out of hiding and go beyond the Barrier."

"It's a trick!" Jared warned. "I've *been* beyond the Barrier. You'll find only Radiation out there!"

"When we were unwise enough to conceal ourselves from the Emissaries, that's what we believed too."

"But the Emissaries are deceiving you! *They're* the ones who turned off the hot springs!"

"Only to make us use our heads and abandon the worlds. That's why they attached patches of Light to the walls. That's why they occasionally left behind the Almighty's Holy Tubular Vessels—so we would be introduced gradually to Light."

Philar pushed past him and the rest of the party followed.

"Come back!" Jared called desperately after them. "You're walking into a trap!"

But they only continued.

He swore and resumed his trek toward the Lower Level, even more vehement in his determination to arm himself for a vengeful assault on Radiation.

Some time later he arrived at the Lower Level with more than a few accumulated scratches and bruises, despite his acquaintance with the passageways closer to his world.

Pausing at the entrance, he let the tension drain out of him like a waning fever. Here was a setting so familiar that he could move confidently about without even using clickstones.

But there was no valid relief, no gentle feeling of homecoming, no elation. The stifling, unnerving curtain of Darkness was pierced only by a barren silence that gave the place an air of incongruity, a tinge of almost hostile strangeness.

Without the central caster sounding its familiar *clacks*, the entire world was a vast, forbidding echo void. He clapped his hands and listened to the awful stillness.

No longer was there the serene gurgling of the hot springs to give literal and audible warmth to his world. And, over there on his left, dying manna plants imposed a crisp, harsh dissonance on the reflections of the *clap*.

Hanging somewhere out there in the Darkness was the violent fear that had coaxed frantic cries of horror from the Forever Man.

Like the Lightlessness itself, Jared could feel the terror closing in on him too. But, wresting his mind back to the task before him, he stepped off briskly for the weapons rack.

He clapped his hands once more to obtain a crude composite of the major landmarks for use as reference points. Then his memory automatically filled in the surface details all about him.

He shouted out in pain when, with his next step, his knee pounded immovable stone. Toppled by his momentum, he went hurtling forward over the obstacle.

He struggled up, massaging his bruised leg. And he swore at the irresponsible Survivor who had violated the Misplacement of Bulky Objects Law. But his anger subsided as he realized that if he had been here when the monsters were decimating the Lower Level, he too would have probably thought of misplacing boulders in the hope that they would serve as hidden obstacles for the invaders.

There was a sound on his right and he spun in that direction. Someone was hidden in a wall fissure, sobbing frantically—a woman. But she had clamped her hands over her mouth to conceal the sounds.

He stepped toward her and she screamed, "No! No! Don't!"

"It's me—Jared."

"Stay away!" she cried. "You're one of them!"

He held back, recognizing Survivoress Glenn, an elderly widow. Helplessly, he listened down at the ground. There was nothing he could do to quell her fears—no reassurance he could offer.

And, sweeping his ears out over this ghost of a world that had been desolated by the monsters, he readily heard the Lower Level was beyond reclamation and would never be lived in again. The demons who had ushered in Doomsperiod had emptied his world of all the meaning it once held.

But now *he* would bring the meaning of vengeance into their infinity! This much he resolved in the name of whatever true Divinity the Survivors had slighted by their devotion to the false Light Almighty.

He spun around and strode grimly for the weapons rack.

"No! Don't go away!" the woman begged. "Don't leave me here for the monsters!"

He sent his hand plunging into the first compartment, fearing for a moment that he would find nothing within. But his anxious fingers closed on a bow and he slung it over his shoulder. That in reprisal for the Lower Level! Two quivers of arrows took their place beside the bow, hanging against his back. Those for Della and the Prime Survivor. A third quiver he strapped across his other shoulder. For Owen!

Reaching into the next compartment, he found a bundle of spears and gathered them under his left arm. For Cyrus, the Thinker! Another sheaf of lances went under his right arm. For Leah and Ethan and the Forever Man!

"Come back!" the woman implored. "Don't leave me here by myself! Don't let the monsters get me!"

She was out of the crevice now and he picked up her sounds as she crawled farther into the world, heading for the entrance so she could cut him off.

Ignoring her, he paused and clapped his hands forcefully for a final hearing of the intimate, for a last indulgence of nostalgia. Then he struck out for the entrance.

He didn't hear the fluttering of wings until the hateful sound was almost upon him. He caught the scent of the soubat at the same time and bolted into frantic action, trying to relieve himself of his excess weapons in time to meet the infuriated charge.

Slipping the quiver straps off his shoulders, he hurled the bow out of his way and dropped one of the bundles of spears. Before he could even begin fumbling with the rope that held together the other sheaf of lances, the soubat hurled itself through the entrance and launched its first onslaught.

Jared dived to one side. He managed to escape the animal's initial pass, suffering only a talon-sliced forearm in the maneuver. Hurling himself on the ground, he again tore at the knot on the bundle of spears.

The soubat's high-pitched shrieks mingled with the terrified cries of the woman, etching every feature of the Lower Level as audibly as though it were the central echo caster itself that was filling the world with sound.

Executing its sweeping turn high against the dome, the marauder plunged down in a second swooping charge. And Jared heard that he couldn't hope to work a spear free before the fanged thing closed in on him.

In the next instant, as he braced himself to receive the beast's full clawing impact, he was abruptly conscious of the Light cone that was darting out of the passageway into the Lower Level.

While it bathed him, it also provided his eyes with the impression of a great, screeching form that was hurtling down in all its fury.

A racking shudder of horror passed through him when he identified the impression as that of the soubat. If the creature had seemed hideous in its audible form, the evil ugliness it conveyed through the medium of Light composites was altogether beyond imagination.

The thing was practically within arm's reach when a tremendous burst of sound roared out of the entrance. At the same time a tiny tongue of odd Light, similar in tone to Hydrogen Himself, lanced into the world.

And Jared sensed that those twin occurrences had something to do with the soubat's going limp in midflight and plummeting to the ground beside him.

Before he could speculate further on the possible coincidence, however, the cone of Light advanced cautiously and he caught the scent of the monster behind it. Using the Light impressions as a guide, he gave the stubborn sheaf of spears a fierce kick and the lances came free, scattering over the ground.

He seized one and, turning toward the entrance, drew it back.

Zip-hiss.

Sharp pain boiled into his chest and the spear clattered to the ground as he stumbled forward and collapsed.

CHAPTER SIXTEEN

AT FIRST JARED THOUGHT HE was receiving touch-sound impressions from Leah. He found himself listening—through the woman's consciousness, he felt certain—to many voices made indistinct by distance. Too, the current of vocal impulses, passing through the "window," flared out to bounce against nearby square walls.

Undoubtedly, the composite was that of the shack in which Leah was being held prisoner. The experience this time, though, was most vivid. He could almost *feel* the straps cutting into the flesh above her elbows as they pinned her arms to the "bed."

"Leah?" he thought.

But there was no response.

Then he realized the perceptions were *not* secondhand. It was *he* who was confined in the shack. And if he hadn't recognized that fact until now, it was possibly because he was still undergoing some of the effects of the *zip-hiss* that had robbed him of his senses.

He listened sharply and determined that there was no one else, human or otherwise, with him. Cautiously, he turned his ears toward the window and heard the rustling of the heavy curtain hanging over that space. A breeze was opening occasional cracks in the folds, through which the voices entered more strongly but still unclearly.

A brisker current caught the curtain, sweeping it partly aside, and he received the sonic impression of a great wall of rock rearing to unguessable heights. It was a composite he was sure he had listened to before and he pressed his memory for the association.

Of course—it was the same wall through which he and Mo-gan had stumbled into Radiation. Before the curtain fluttered back into place, he even heard the remote hollowness of the passageway's gaping end as it flared out on infinity.

There was no doubt about it now. He was somewhere in the terrifying vastness of Radiation. His eyes opened and he flinched before the onslaught of impressions. Yet, the sensation was not as fierce as he had expected. And he supposed its mildness was due to the fact that the walls of the shack were keeping out most of the Light.

His head rolled toward the window but snapped instantly back. In the split beat before his lids had clamped shut he had gotten a frightening impression. It was as though part of Hydro-gen had leaped in through a rift in the curtain to cast Himself in a long, narrow streak on the relative Darkness of the floor!

Many beats later he forced his eyes open again and began struggling against his bonds. His arms, free below the elbows, thrashed upward as far as they could, but to no avail. Against the lingering aftereffects of the *zip-hiss* he was still powerless.

In the next moment he stifled a fearful cry and brought trembling lids back down over his eyes. He had received the composite of something menacing and horrible—right there before him! Something bulbous with five curving protuberances that reminded him vaguely of the sonic impression of a—

But, no, it *couldn't* be! Yet—

He opened his eyes and experimentally wiggled a finger on his left hand. And one of the protuberances on the bulbous thing wiggled too. Relieved, he lowered the hand. But he was even more puzzled. The legends had said Light would touch all things and bring incredibly refined impressions. None of the beliefs, however, had even hinted that a Survivor might receive composites of *his own* body!

He brought the hand back up where he could *see* it and studied the impressions. How unbelievably perfect they were! Why, he could recognize each individual crease in the palm, each hair on the back!

Then he tensed in stark disbelief. The hand had abruptly split into two, as though the original had given birth to another just like it! The two drifted back into one, then separated again, moving further apart!

At the same time he was aware of a shifting pressure on the muscles of his eyeballs—a tenseness that crossed the bridge of his nose whenever the hand divided, then relaxed again as the parts rejoined. And he found that with concentration he could prevent the confusing and certainly false impression of two members when all his other senses told him there could be only one.

Voices in the immediate vicinity of the shack put Jared on guard and he had time to feign an attitude of sleep before he heard the door open. Listening to two of his captors enter, he remained rigid as they came over and stood by the bed. And as they spoke he could hear their words filtering through the cloth face masks:

"This the new one?"

"The last brought out. Incidentally, as best we can determine, he's the one who slugged Hawkins over that infrared-sensitive girl."

"Oh, *that* one. Fenton—Jared Fenton. His old man's been waiting for this day."

"Want me to go tell Evan we got him?"

"Can't. He's been moved to advanced reconditioning."

Jared hoped the pair hadn't detected his start at the mention of his father. Convincing them he was asleep was his only hope of forestalling torture.

"Well, Thorndyke," said the closer of the two, "let's get on with it."

Jared couldn't help starting again on learning Thorndyke Himself was there.

"Has he had his primary shots yet?" the latter asked.

"All of them."

"Then I guess we can shuck these without touching off another cold epidemic."

Jared heard them remove the cloths from their faces. Then a hand came down unexpectedly on his shoulder.

"All right, Fenton," Thorndyke said. "I'm going to hit you between the eyes with a lot of stuff you won't even understand—at first. But it'll seep through gradually."

When Jared didn't answer, the other captor asked, "You suppose he's still out?"

"Of course not. All those who don't bounce up screaming put on the sleep act. Come on, Fenton. As I get it, you've had more experience with light than any of them. You ought to take this in stride."

Perhaps it was the calculated smoothness of the voice. Or, it may have been that, without realizing it, Jared had grown tired of holding his eyes shut. At any rate, in the next beat light was pouring into his conscious and carrying a succession of inseparable impressions with it.

"That's better," Thorndyke sighed. *"Now* we're moving."

But Jared's lids flicked shut, blocking out the disturbing sensations. And he compared the Light composite he had stored in that brief instant with the audible impulses he was still receiving.

Thorndyke was a big man (briefly, he questioned his description of the monster as human) with a blunt face whose bone structure suggested strength and determination. Those traits, however, were a puzzling contrast to the femininity implied by his hairless chin.

Loose folds of cloth that fluttered with each minor movement confused the overall composite. But Jared conceded that, for beings who lived in the vastness and relative warmth of infinity, tight-fitting cloths would be both uncomfortable and inconvenient.

"Throw back those drapes, Caseman," Thorndyke said, "and let's get some light in here."

"You sure he's ready for it?" the other asked, going over to the window.

"I think so. He's holding up almost as well as a Zivver. Probably had more brushes with light than we know about."

A surge of apprehension shuddered through Jared as he listened to the curtain being drawn aside and sensed the assault of fierce light against his closed lids.

Thorndyke's hand came back to rest on his shoulder. "Easy now, Fenton. Nothing's going to hurt you."

But, of course, it was only deceit. They were going to soften him, give him a false sense of confidence. Then, when they smothered his hope with torture, their amusement would be complete.

He opened his eyes. But he could hardly brave the fury of light pouring into the shack now. When he relowered his lids, however, it wasn't as much because he feared the light as it was because he had seen *two* Thorndykes standing side by side! It made him tremble.

Thorndyke laughed. "Lack of optical co-ordination makes things confusing, doesn't it? But you'll learn the finer points of focusing sooner or later."

He drew up a framework bench and sat beside the bed. "Let's set a few things straight for the record. Some of it will go over your head. The rest will rub against logic. Take whatever you can on faith. You'll get it all eventually. First—this is *not* Radiation. We're *not* demons. You're *not* dead and lost on the way to Paradise. In the sky outside is the sun. It's quite an impressive thing, but it's *not* Hydrogen Himself."

"It's not Light Almighty either," Caseman added.

"No, Fenton," Thorndyke affirmed. "Contrary to what you believe now, you may later start thinking of this outside world as Paradise."

"Actually," said Caseman, "you'll learn to conceive of Paradise in another way—yet unattainable in a material sense, still beyond infinity, but beyond a new kind of infinity. Which leads up to the fact that you're going to have to trade in a bunch of old beliefs for new ones."

There was a moment of silence that played heavily against Jared's patience. Then Thorndyke asked, "You still with us? Want to say anything?"

"I want to go back to my Level," Jared managed without opening his eyes.

"There!" Caseman laughed. "He *does* talk!"

"I *thought* you'd want to go back," Thorndyke said wearily. "Can't be done. However, how about this: Would you like to, ah, hear—what's the girl's name?"

"Della," Caseman supplied.

Jared strained against his bonds. "What are you doing with her? Can I—*see* her?"

"Say! This one even knows what he's *doing* with his eyes! Caseman, what about the girl? How's she making out?"

"Taking things in stride like the other Zivvers, since sight isn't completely alien to them. Of course, she doesn't understand what it's all about. But she's willing to accept things as they are for the moment."

Thorndyke slapped his thigh. "All right, Fenton. You'll see the girl tomorrow—next period."

There it was—the beginning of the torture. Offer him something, then tantalize him by holding it just out of his reach.

"So much for the preliminaries," Thorndyke said finally. "Now, here's a whole bunch of facts you can file away against the time when they'll all start making sense:

"Your two levels and the Zivver group are descendants of U.S. Survival Complex Number Eleven. Consider a whole world—not the kind you know, but one many, many times greater with billions—you know what a billion is?—billions of people crammed in it. They're divided into two camps, ready to hurl themselves at one another with weapons deadly beyond imagination. Even to use them would mean to, ah—poison all the air for many generations."

Thorndyke paused and Jared got the impression it was a story he had told hundreds of times.

"This war *does* start," he resumed, "but, fortunately, not until preparations are made for the survival of a few groups—seventeen, to be exact. Sanctuaries are established beneath the ground and are sealed off against the poisoned atmosphere."

"Actually," Caseman put in, "even making it possible for a handful to survive was a remarkable achievement. It wouldn't have been possible without adaptation of nuclear power and development of a type of plant life that functioned through thermosynthesis instead of photo—"

The flow of words came to a halt, as though Caseman had sensed his listener's inability to cope with them.

"Manna plants to you," Thorndyke explained curtly. "At any rate, the survival complexes were prepared; the war started, and the selected few fled from their—Paradise, so to speak. For the most part, things went along as planned. All equipment worked properly; knowledge and familiar institutions were preserved, and life went on with everybody knowing where they were and why they were there. Generations later, after the outside air had purged itself, the descendants of the original survivors determined it was safe to return outside."

"Except in Complex Eleven," Caseman amended. "There, things didn't go smoothly."

"Indeed they didn't," Thorndyke agreed. "Let's back up, though. From what I hear, Fenton, you're a nonbeliever—never accepted the idea light was God. By now you probably even have a pretty good idea just what it really is, even though you're stubborn as hell about opening your eyes. At any rate, we'll take it from there:

"Light is as natural a thing as, say, the sound from a waterfall. In its primary form it comes in abundance from what you'll swear is Hydrogen Himself when you see it. We also have ways of producing it artificially, as you know by now. And each of the survival complexes had their own light-producing systems right up until the time they were able to return to the outside world."

Caseman, leaning closer to the bed, interrupted, "Except yours. After a few generations you lost your ability to maintain those systems should anything happen. And something *did* happen."

"There was a minor fault shift," Thorndyke resumed. "And—well, the lights went out. At the same time most of the superheated water conduits leading to your basic chamber were snapped off. Your people had to push farther into the complex, occupying other chambers that were partly prepared to receive possible population overflows."

Vaguely, Jared was beginning to construct a composite of what they *wanted* him to believe. But it was so incredible—the parts he *could* understand—that logic revolted against it. For instance, who could comprehend all infinity jammed with hostile people? Yet, there had been nothing menacing in either Thorndyke's or Caseman's voices. As a matter of fact, the words, though meaningless for the most part, were soothing in their own way.

But no! That was *just* the reaction they were *trying* to get out of him! They were using trickery to gain his confidence. Nevertheless, he was determined they wouldn't break his resolve to free himself and find Della so they could escape from Radiation.

He opened his eyes, but let them linger only briefly on Thorndyke's composite. To one side of that central impression he could see the window with its drapes drawn back. Beyond reared the huge wall of rock and earth with its gaping hole of darkness that was the mouth of the passageways.

Then he tensed as the light impressions achieved even more clarity. Off in the distance were scores of moving figures—figures he was certain were either Survivors or monsters, but which were *no bigger than his little finger!* And he also saw now that the mouth of the corridor leading back to his world was as small as the nail on that finger!

Caseman must have gotten a composite of his face twisting with dismay. "What's wrong with him, Thorndyke?"

But the other only laughed. "He's having his first experience with perception. Don't be afraid, Fenton. You'll get used to things in the distance seeming small. Aren't voices closer to you louder than those far away?"

"He can see pretty well for a beginner," Caseman offered.

"I'd say he's even several leaps ahead of the others at this point. He's probably been outside before now. That right, Fenton?"

But Jared didn't answer. Eyes closed, he was bemoaning the fact that the horrors of infinity were even more awful than he had suspected. He *had* to get back to his own worlds!

"About Survival Complex Eleven—" Thorndyke interrupted his anxious thoughts. "When your people left their basic chamber they left knowledge and reason behind. We found that out after we broke the seal and made our first trip into the passages. Incidentally, we're members of an expedition from Survival Complex Seven, released from our caves almost a generation ago. As I was saying, we happened upon a lone Survivor in one of your corridors. After I finally managed to get a half nelson on him, we pretty much guessed what the score was."

"That was an Upper Level Survivor," Caseman noted. "It took weeks to pound some logic into his head. At the same time we realized that getting the rest of you out under the sun wouldn't be a simple matter of walking up and saying, 'Here we are and this is light and let's go outside.'"

"That's right," Thorndyke affirmed. "Until we could study the situation, we had to take it slow, collaring a Survivor at a time, while we mapped the general layout. We couldn't move in in force until we knew all the niches and crannies you would hide in if we should scare you out of your chambers."

Some of the account was making sense now and Jared forced himself to lie back and listen.

Thorndyke rose and laughed briefly. "We had planned to educate a few Survivors to the facts and let them go back inside, without light, to break the news gently to the others."

"Wouldn't work though," Caseman disclosed. "After one of you fellows gets used to using his eyes, he finds he can't get around in the dark *without* light. Most of them are even afraid to go back."

Thorndyke rubbed his hands together. "That ought to be enough for the time being, Fenton. Think it over. I've an idea that the next time around you'll have some questions to ask. To help answer them, we'll bring along some people you know and trust."

Jared reopened his eyes in time to see them leaving the shack. And he noted, to his consternation, that they had been right about that matter of perspective at least. The farther away they got, the smaller they became.

He strained desperately against his bonds, but to no avail. Then, pausing to rest, he turned his head toward the opposite wall. Instantly a great flood of intense light bored into his eyes and he cried out in dismay. Screaming at him from one corner of the window was an edge of that great disc which Thorndyke had denied was Hydrogen! Was it maneuvering toward his shack—trying to come in after him?

Frantically, he threw all his strength into a final attempt to release himself. The bonds snapped and flew off, even as he felt the heat of that—sun, Thorndyke had called it, intensifying against his back.

He lunged for the door and clawed unavailingly at the solid curtain until his fingernails cracked. After a moment of hesitancy, he sprinted across the floor and hurled himself through the window.

Landing on his feet, he saw that the sun was not as close as he had feared. But there were other complications. The impressions entering his eyes told him his shack was merely one in a row. Only, each successive shack was a little smaller than the one immediately preceding it, until the last was scarcely bigger than his hand!

Moreover, all those people he had seen and heard in the distance were shouting and racing toward him. And, even though they were shorter than his finger, the closer they came the taller they grew!

Confounded, he turned and raced up the incline toward the towering wall of earth that embraced the passageway entrance.

"Survivor on the loose! Survivor on the loose!" was the cry that rose behind him.

He stumbled over a minor obstacle he hadn't heard and scrambled bewildered to his feet. The heat from that great thing called the "sun" beat mercilessly down on his bare shoulders and back as he groped his way up the incline, working ever closer to the mouth of the corridor.

The gaping hole of darkness split in two and the parts drifted away from each other as he swore at his eye muscles, trying to force strength into them. Eventually, the pair of holes flowed back into one and stood out more distinctly as he drew up before the mouth of the passageway, gasping for breath.

But he *couldn't* force himself to push on into the tunnel!

The darkness was too thick and threatening!

There could be a soubat waiting around the first bend!

Or he might plunge into an unfathomable pit which he would neither see nor hear!

With his pursuers almost upon him, he spun impulsively and raced off alongside the immense wall of rock. He stumbled repeatedly and, at one point, found himself rolling down a steep incline until a thick growth of low, rough plants checked his momentum.

He thrashed through the insubstantial obstruction and pushed on, running half the time with his eyes closed and crashing into the broad stems of the Paradise plants that were in his way. But, at least, the voices behind him were becoming more distant and the heat of Hydrogen on his arms and back was not as severe as it had been for innumerable beats.

He ran and paused for breath and ran again and again until finally he fell and rolled helplessly down through another stretch of plants that hugged the ground. When he came to a halt he scurried farther into the thick growth and lay there exhausted, his face pressed against moist earth.

CHAPTER SEVENTEEN

"I GUESS I WAS WRONG, Jared. It's not really all that horrible. And, besides, I think maybe the monsters might be trying to help us after all."

There was a quality to Leah's thoughts that had been noticeably absent the last few times she had made contact. Now her unspoken words were calm, ordered. It was as though Thorndyke, after somehow breaking her resistance, had established complete control and was using the woman as a lure, Jared imagined.

"No, Jared—it's not like that at all. At least, I don't think so. I'm sure they're not making me do this."

If they were, Jared assured himself, then the monsters were even more treacherous than he had imagined.

"They may not be monsters at all," she went on. *"They really haven't hurt me, except to force my eyes open to the light. And I've been in contact with Ethan. He's not afraid at all! He even thinks they're good."*

Jared rolled over and, though still more asleep than awake, recalled that he had fallen exhausted somewhere out among the low, thick growth of infinity.

"Ethan is satisfied," she offered, *"because he can get around without help from me, without even having to use his pouch of crickets for echoes. He says he doesn't have to hear when he can see what's before him."*

A startling sound erupted somewhere above him and Jared stiffened against the coarse, damp ground. Even

though it had been frightening at first, there was a strange en-
chantment to the trio of sharp, shrill notes that filled infinity
with a plaintive pride and forced back the audible emptiness.

"Don't be afraid," Leah encouraged, *evidently having heard the
beautiful tones through his ears. "I've listened to it many times. It was
one of the things that finally made me decide this* can't *be Radiation."*

"What is it?" he asked as he listened again to the piercingly
sweet succession of high, low, and medium notes.

*"It's a winged animal—a bird." Then, as she detected his apprehen-
sion, "No—nothing like a soubat. It's a small delicate thing. Ethan
says it's one of the original creatures of infinity—the 'outside world,' he
calls it—that managed to survive."*

*When he said nothing she went on, "It's what they call 'night' out
there now. But it'll end soon and day will return. Ethan says they
have to find you before Hydrogen comes up."*

He was aware of a persistent itching, a stinging along his
shoulders and back. It was not an intense sensation, but it was
disturbing enough to bring him completely and uncomfortably
awake.

He opened his eyes and his fingers dug tensely into the soft
earth.

There was no great fury of light all around him as there had
been before! Now there was only a softness which was pleasing
to the eye and drove home the welcome realization that things
didn't have to be all light or darkness out here, that there could
be an in-between.

The three distinct notes sounded again and he caught their
subtle reflections from the stems of the Paradise plants that
reared all around him. But out there above the lacy tops of the
plants—"trees," he reminded himself—the entrancing notes lost
themselves in the vastness overhead.

And now, as his eyes bored out beyond those fragile treetops,
he saw a great disc of cool light that was both like and unlike the
sun. It was the same size as the latter. But, whereas Hydrogen
was as furious as the sound of a thousand roaring cataracts, this
sphere was gentle and captivating, bringing to mind the win-
some notes of the winged creature.

His eyes swept the great dome covering this infinity and, breathless, he gave up trying to count the lively little points of light that danced around up there and became stronger or weaker as he studied them.

Beyond and between the gay motes of the dome was a somber darkness that reminded him of the corridors and worlds in which he had spent all his life up until now. But the fascinating bits of light were so elegant that the eye found little time to concern itself with the intervening darkness.

A world without a material boundary, save for the flat ground underneath him. And, enclosing that world, not an infinity of rocks and mud, but an infinity of semidarkness enlivened by pleasant points and a graceful disc of light—at the moment. At other times, it was an infinity of bold, loud light dominated by a great, harsh thing called the "sun."

"A new kind of infinity," Caseman had said.

And indeed it was. A new kind of infinity with tremendous, novel concepts—so different that the language he knew couldn't begin to contain it.

Despite his restrained sense of wonder, he could not hold back a feeling of despair. Now, with the light around him less intense than it had ever been since he was brought to this outside world, he knew he could never again tolerate the pitch darkness of the passages and Levels. He drew back from himself, surprised over the frank admission that he hadn't the courage to return to his familiar worlds. Did that mean he would have to stay out here among the incomprehensible things of infinity for the rest of his life?

"I'm afraid so, Jared." Leah's silent words were a sober affirmation. "I've—looked into many minds during this last period. Most of us realize the inner worlds are a thing of the past."

He sat up sharply. If he was receiving Leah's thoughts while he was awake, then she couldn't be too far from him! But before he could question her, he became almost painfully aware of the irritating sensation along his shoulders and arms. And when he scratched the skin there it felt as though it were boiling.

The bird shrilled its blithesome notes again and he listened to the mellow tones impart their aesthetic quality to the pleasant things before his eyes. It was all charming, this bizarre setting—not beautiful in the way that fine sound appealed to the ear, but gracious in the sensations of form and shape and the variations of light and darkness that came to his eyes.

He became gradually conscious, however, of a disturbing element out there in infinity and he turned his head apprehensively toward it. One section of the dome, far out beyond the treetops, was casting off its darkness. An even flow of light was creeping up from the ground to swallow the points of light that were already up there.

Leah had implied that the present period of "night" was only temporary, that Hydrogen would be back to cast his fury of light over everything. Could this be the end of the calm phase he had been experiencing?

He rose, trembling, and backed away from the light-smeared portion of the dome, forcing his way through the low growth.

But he started and his head snapped to the right as he saw another kind of light out there between the stems of the Paradise plants—a swinging cone that could only signify the approach of Thorndyke or one of his other captors!

From overhead the sharp notes of the bird stabbed once more into the semi-light and Jared tried desperately to sort out the returning echoes. But, besides hearing that there were actually *four* persons hidden in the void behind the light cone, he could squeeze no details out of the reflected sound.

He ducked back down into the thick growth, listening intensely to the group draw closer and hoping that the minor plants around him would prevent the light impressions from betraying his presence.

A breeze sprung up and he tensed as all the lacy plant tops as far as he could hear began whispering and swaying. Coming generally from the direction in which he was facing, the gently moving air currents brought the scents of his pursuers.

Thorndyke was among them, which in itself wasn't surprising. Even though he had been in the presence of the man only once before, he easily recognized his personal odor.

But mingled with that scent were three other unmistakable ones—

Ethan!

Owen!

Della!

He could believe that these beings of infinity had had plenty of time to bend Owen and Ethan to their purpose. But certainly not Della! She had been out here only half a period longer than he!

"*The girl's a Zivver, Jared,*" *Leah pointed out.* "*She must understand these things much more easily than you or I.*"

Ignoring the unsolicited thoughts, he backed off through the low plants, making as little noise as possible. On his left, more light had splashed itself against the distant dome and he was certain now that he was seeing the imminent coming of the dreadful sun.

"*Jared, don't run off—please! Stay where you are!*"

It was Ethan's thoughts, relayed by Leah, that intruded on his conscious this time. That could only mean Ethan and Leah and even Thorndyke must be working together!

"*Yes, Jared,*" *she admitted.* "*I helped Ethan reach you. He knows what's best. He says that if they don't get you back in the shack soon you're going to be sick.*"

"*No, not Radiation sickness,*" *Ethan quickly assured.* "*Sickness from being in the sunlight too long without being used to it. And other ailments too—ailments Thorndyke wants to protect you from.*"

Then Ethan's voice came audibly, in an aside that obviously hadn't been intended for Jared's ears: "He's right up there—in that thicket."

Jared sprang from concealment and hesitated for a moment while the intense light from Thorndyke's caster stabbed into his eyes and prevented him from seeing anything else. Then he whirled to lunge away.

"You wanted to find light, didn't you?" Owen called out sharply. "And now that you've found it you're acting like a squeamish old woman."

Pausing uncertainly, Jared listened to the familiar voice that he hadn't heard in many periods—since before the monsters had crossed the Barrier. But it was what Owen had said, rather than the surprise of hearing his voice, that had had the arresting effect.

It was true. He *had* spent his whole life searching for light. And all along he had allowed for the possibility that, when he found it, it might be completely unnatural, utterly incomprehensible, frightening.

He had found it. But he had only quailed and tried to hide from his own discovery.

Maybe this infinity—this outside world—might not be so terrifying if he would only give himself the chance to understand it.

"I *could* shoot you an injection from here." It was Thorndyke's calm voice that reached out to him through the semi-light. "But I'm counting on you to respond to reason."

Yet, as the steady cone of light advanced, Jared backed involuntarily away from it.

His skin was irritating him persistently now and he felt a grimace spread over his face as his hands went up to rub the boiling surface of his arms and shoulders.

"Don't let it bother you too much," Owen laughed reassuringly. "You're just having your first run-in with sunburn. We'll fix it up if you'll just come back."

Then, as though aware of what was in his mind, Thorndyke said, "*Of course* there are things you don't understand. Just as there are things about this outside world not even *we* know."

The light cone stabbed beyond the tenuous treetops. "For instance," Thorndyke's voice followed the motion of the light caster, "we don't know what's out there. And, when we find out, we still won't know what's beyond it all. Infinity's still infinity—in your cave world as well as in this one. Eternity's eternity. Those are some of the barriers, some of the unknowables."

Somehow Jared didn't feel as helpless, as insignificant as he once had before these beings of the outside world. Thorndyke had called the sprawling region within that towering wall of rock and earth a "cave world." But, in many respects, this greater creation was merely a greater cave. One that also had a dome and an infinity beyond that dome and a curtain of darkness separating all the knowable from all the unknowable.

A figure stepped boldly into the cone of light—a tiny human figure. But he wasn't alarmed. He knew it would grow in size as it approached—until it reached normal proportions.

Calmly now, he watched the figure advance, briefly aware that a light greater than that coming from Thorndyke's caster was falling upon it. This could only be the light which was intensifying along the edge of the dome behind him.

Another breeze rippled and whispered through the Paradise trees and the personal scent of Della came along with it, clear and strong.

"I don't understand any of these things either," she said, advancing, "but I'm willing to wait and ziv what happens."

And a satisfying realization unfolded against the background of his current experience: Zivving and seeing were *so much* alike that, out here, the physical difference between him and Della was negligible. There was no longer any reason for him to feel inferior.

His attention remained steadily on her as she came closer. Overhead, the bird sang its delightful song and the poignant beauty of the refrain strengthened the appreciation his eyes felt for the girl as she drew up before him.

The delicate, refined impressions he was receiving of Della struck him as being soft as the music of the melodious tones, vibrant like the mighty voice of a great waterfall muffled into modesty by distance.

She extended her hand and he clasped it.

"We'll stay out here and see what happens—together," Jared said, heading back toward Thorndyke and the others.

♈

CPSIA information can be obtained
at www.ICGtesting.com
Printed in the USA
JSHW030726130922
30352JS00001B/1